Decision made, Zahir took hold of Annalina's arm.

"You will accompany me back to the party. We will seek out the king and tell him what has happened. Then we will announce your engagement."

"Didn't you understand a word I said?" The fight was back in her eyes. "The king won't marry me now. That's the reason I just kissed you in full view of that photographer."

"We will announce your engagement, not to the king but to his brother, the prince."

"Yeah, great idea! I take it you must be employed more for your brawn than your brains." Zahir felt every muscle in his body stiffen at her mocking gibe. He was going to enjoy punishing her for her insolence. "The prince is hardly going to want to marry me, either, is he?"

"As of five minutes ago, the prince has no choice."

Narrowing his eyes, Zahir watched defiance turn to confusion then to a creeping realization. A strangely perverse sense of pleasure stole over him.

Her trembling hand flew to her mouth then made a fist as she stuffed it between her lips, biting down onto her knuckles to stifle her cry.

"Ah, yes, Princess, I see the truth is dawning." Zahir threw back his shoulders, almost enjoying himself. "I am Zahir Zahani, Prince of Nabatean, brother of King Rashid. And as of five minutes ago, your future husband."

Wedlocked!

Conveniently wedded, passionately bedded!

Whether there's a debt to be paid, a will to be obeyed or a business to be saved... she's got no choice but to say "I do!"

But these billionaire bridegrooms have got another think coming if they imagine marriage will be that easy...

Soon their convenient brides become the object of an *inconvenient* desire!

Find out what happens after the vows in

The Billionaire's Defiant Acquisition
by Sharon Kendrick

One Night to Wedding Vows
by Kim Lawrence

Wedded, Bedded, Betrayed
by Michelle Smart

Expecting a Royal Scandal
by Caitlin Crews

Trapped by Vialli's Vows
by Chantelle Shaw

Baby of His Revenge
by Jennie Lucas

A Diamond for Del Rio's Housekeeper
by Susan Stephens

Look out for more **Wedlocked!** stories coming soon!

Andie Brock

BOUND BY HIS DESERT DIAMOND

ISBN-13: 978-0-373-21308-5

Bound by His Desert Diamond

First North American Publication 2016

This edition published by arrangement with Harlequin Books S.A.

For questions and comments about the quality of this book, please contact us at CustomerService@Harlequin.com.

Printed in U.S.A.

Andie Brock started inventing imaginary friends around the age of four and is still doing that today—only now the sparkly fairies have made way for spirited heroines and sexy heroes. Thankfully, she now has some real friends, as well as a husband and three children, plus a grumpy but lovable cat. Andie lives in Bristol and when not actually writing might well be plotting her next passionate romance story.

Books by Andie Brock

Harlequin Presents

The Sheikh's Wedding Contract
The Last Heir of Monterrato

One Night With Consequences

The Shock Cassano Baby

Visit Harlequin.com for more titles.

To Roger. Who has spent far more time discussing manly emotions and reactions and romance in general than he ever signed up for! Thank you, Con. x

CHAPTER ONE

CLASPING THE COLD metal railings, Annalina stared down at the swirling black depths of the River Seine. She shivered violently, her heart thumping beneath the tight-fitting bodice of her evening gown, her designer shoes biting into the soft flesh of her heels. Clearly they had not been designed for a mad sprint down the bustling boulevards and cobbled back streets of Paris.

Oh, God. Anna dragged in a shuddering lung full of cold night air. *What had she just done?*

Somewhere behind her in one of Paris's most grand hotels, a society party was in swing. A glittering, star-studded occasion attended by royalty and heads of state, the great, the good and the glamorous from the world over. It was a party being thrown in her honour. And worse, far worse, a party where a man she had only just met was about to announce that she was to be his bride.

She let out a rasping breath, watching the cloud of condensation disperse into the night. She had no idea where she was or what she was going to do now but she did know that there was no going back. The brutal fact was she couldn't go through with this marriage, no matter what the consequences. Right up until tonight she had genuinely believed she could do it, could commit to this union, to please her father and to save her country from financial ruin.

Even yesterday, when she had met her intended for the first time, she had played along. Watching in a kind of dazed stupor as the ring had been slipped onto her finger, a perfunctory gesture performed by a man who had just wanted to get the deed over with, and witnessed by her father, whose steely-eyed glare had left no room for second thoughts or doubts. As King of the small country of Dorrada he was going to make sure that this union took place. That his daughter would marry King Rashid Zahani, ruler of the recently reformed Kingdom of Nabatean, if it was the last thing she ever did.

Which frankly, right now, looked like a distinct possibility. Anna gazed down at the ring on her finger. The enormous diamond glittered back at her, mocking her with its ostentatious sparkle. Heaven only knew what it was worth—enough to pay the entire annual salaries of the palace staff, no doubt, and with money to spare. She tugged it over her cold knuckles and held it in her palm, feeling the burden of its weight settle like a stone in her heart.

To hell with it.

Closing her fist, she raised herself up on tiptoes, leaning as far over the railings as she could. She was going to do this. She was going to fling this hateful ring into the river. She was going to control her own destiny.

He came from out of nowhere—an avalanche of heat, weight and muscle that landed on top of her, knocking the breath from her lungs, flattening her against the granite wall of his chest. She could see nothing except the darkness of him, feel nothing except the strength of the arms that were locked around her like corded steel. Her body went limp, her bones dissolving with shock. Only her poor heart tried to keep her alive, taking up a wild, thundering beat.

'Oh, no, you don't.'

He growled the words over the top of her head, somewhere in the outside world that, until a couple of moments ago, she had quite taken for granted. Now she panicked she would never see it again.

Don't what?

Anna forced her oxygen-starved brain to work out what he meant. Shouldn't it be her telling this mad man what he shouldn't be doing? Like crushing her so hard against him that she was almost asphyxiated. She tried to move inside his grip but the ring of steel tightened still further, pinning her arms to her sides. Her mouth, she suddenly registered, was pressed against flesh. She could touch him with the tip of her tongue, taste the very masculine mix of spice and sweat. She could feel the coarseness of what had to be chest hair against her lips. Forcing her mouth open, she bared her teeth, then brought them down as hard as she could. *Yes!* Her sharp nip connected with a small but significant ridge of his flesh. She felt him buck, then curse loudly in a foreign tongue.

'Why, you little…' Releasing her just enough to be able to see her face, her captor glared at her with ferociously piercing black eyes. 'What the hell are you? Some sort of animal?'

'Me!' Incredulity spiked through the terror as Anna stared back at him, squinting through the dark shadows to try and work out who the hell he was, what the hell he wanted. He seemed somehow familiar but she couldn't pull back far enough to see. 'You call me an animal when you've just leapt out on me from the shadows like some sort of crazed beast!' The jet-black eyes narrowed, glinting with all the menace of a brandished blade. Perhaps it wasn't such a good idea to goad him. 'Look.' She tried for what she hoped was a conciliatory tone, though her voice was too muffled from being squeezed half to death to be able to tell. 'If it's money you want, I'm afraid I don't have any.'

This much was true. She had fled the party without even thinking to snatch up her clutch bag.

'I don't want your money.'

The rush of fear returned. Oh, God, what did he want, then? Terror closed her throat as she desperately tried to come up with something to distract him. Suddenly she remembered the ring that was still digging into her palm. It was worth a try. 'I do have a ring, though—right here in my hand.' She tried unsuccessfully to free her arm to show it to him. 'If you let me go you can have it.'

This produced a mocking snort from above her.

'No, really, it's worth thousands—millions, for all I know.'

'I know exactly what it's worth.'

He did? Anna gasped with relief. So that was what this brute was after—the wretched ring.

Well, he was welcome to it. Good riddance. She just wished she could get out of her engagement as easily. She was struggling to thrust it upon him when he spoke again.

'I should do. I signed the cheque.'

Anna stilled. *What?* This wasn't making any sense. Who on earth was this guy? Twisting in his arms, she felt his grip loosen a fraction, enough to let her straighten her spine, tip her chin and gaze into his face. Her heart thundered at what she saw.

Fearsomely handsome features glowered down at her, all sharp-angled planes of chiselled cheekbones, a blade-straight nose and an uncompromising jut of a granite-hewn jaw, all highlighted by the orange glow of the Victorian street lights. He exuded strength and power, and his sheer forcefulness shivered its way through Anna's body, settling somewhere deep within her core.

She recognised him now. She remembered having seen him out of the corner of her eye somewhere amid the flurry of guests at the party, amid the endless introductions and polite conversations. A dark yet unmissable figure, he had been looming in the background, taking in everything—taking in her, too, before she had haughtily turned her profile to him. Some sort of bodyguard or minder—that was who he had to be. She remembered now the way he had hovered at the side of Rashid Zahani, her new fiancé, always a step behind him but somehow in charge, controlling him, owning the space, the glittering ballroom and everyone in it.

But a bodyguard who picked out engagement rings?

Somehow she couldn't see this towering force of a man lingering over a tray of jewels. Not that that mattered. What mattered was that he took his brutish hands off her and left her alone to carry on making the hideous mess of her life that she seemed so hell-bent on doing.

'So, if I am not being mugged, perhaps you would be kind enough to tell me exactly why you have leapt out of the dark and scared me half to death. And why you're not letting me go now, this instant. Presumably you know who I am?'

'Indeed I do, *Princess*.'

The word 'princess' hissed through his teeth, curdling something in Anna's stomach. Loosening his arms from around her back, he moved his hands to her shoulders, where they weighed down on her with searing heat.

'And, in reply to your question, I'm stopping you from doing something extremely foolish.'

'Flinging this into the river, you mean?' With

a contemptuous toss of her head, Anna opened her hand to reveal the hated ring.

'That and yourself along with it.'

'Myself?' She scowled up at him. 'You don't mean…? You didn't think..?'

'That you were about to leap to your death? Yes.'

'And why exactly would I want to do that?'

'You tell me, Princess. You flee from your own engagement party in a state of high anxiety, position yourself on a bridge with a thirty-foot drop into a fast-flowing river and then lean forward in an extremely dangerous way. What was I supposed to think?'

'You weren't supposed to think at all. You were supposed to mind your own business and leave me alone.'

'Ah, but this *is* my business. *You* are my business.'

A wave of heat swept over Anna at the possessiveness of his words.

'Well, fine.' She fought to stand her ground. 'Now you can go back to your boss and tell him that you prevented a suicide that was never going to happen by leaping on an innocent woman—a woman who just happens to be a princess, may I remind you?—and scaring her half to death. I'm sure he will be very pleased with you.'

Piercingly dark eyes held hers, flicking over her like the flames of a newly lit fire, mesmerising with a promise of deadly heat. There was something else there too, an amused arrogance, if Anna wasn't mistaken. If 'amused' could ever be used to describe those forbidding features.

'In fact I may decide to press charges.' Anger hardened her voice. 'If you don't get your hands off me within the next second, I will make sure everyone knows of your behaviour.' She jerked at her shoulders to try and dislodge his leaden hold.

'I'll take my hands off you when I am good and ready.' His voice was as dark and menacing as the river that flowed beneath them. 'And when I do it will be to personally escort you back to the party. There are a number of very important people there waiting for a big announcement, in case you had forgotten.'

'No, not forgotten.' Anna swallowed. 'But, as it happens, I've changed my mind. I've decided I won't be marrying King Rashid after all. In fact, perhaps you would like to go back and inform him of my decision.'

'Ha!' A cruel laugh escaped his lips. 'I can assure you, you will be doing no such thing. You will accompany me back to the ballroom and you will act as if nothing has happened.

The engagement will be announced as planned. The wedding will go ahead as planned.'

'I think you are forgetting yourself.' Anna fired back at him. 'You are in no position to speak to me like that.'

'I'll speak to you any way I want, Princess. And you will do as I say. You can start by putting that ring back on your finger.' His hand moved to Anna's, picking up the ring and sending a jolt of awareness through her. For one crazy moment, she thought he was going to slip it back on her finger himself, like some sort of deranged suitor, but instead he handed it to her and waited as she did as she was told, the sheer force of his presence giving her no choice other than to obey.

With her ring in place, he took hold of her arm with manacle-like force and Anna found herself being turned away from the railings, presumably to be marched back to the party. This was outrageous. How dared he treat her like this? She wanted to spell out in the clearest possible terms that she did not take orders from bodyguards, or ring-choosers, or whoever this arrogant piece of work thought he was. But presumably he was working on the orders of King Rashid…

With her mind racing in all directions, she tried to think what on earth she could do—how she could get herself out of this mess. Physically trying to get away from him was clearly not an option. Even if she managed to escape his iron grip—which was highly unlikely, as the forceful fingers wrapped around her cold skin could testify—she would never be able to run fast enough to get away from him. The image of him chasing and finally capturing her flailing body was strangely erotic, given the circumstances.

She would have to use the only thing she had left in her armoury—her feminine wiles. Drawing herself up to her full height, she let her shoulder blades slide down her back, which had the desired effect of pushing her chest forward, accentuating the fullness of her breasts as they spilled over the tight bodice of her gown. Ah, yes, she had his attention now. She felt her nipples harden beneath his veiled scrutiny, sensing rather than witnessing his eyes delve into the valley of her cleavage. Her breath stalled in her throat, a tingling warmth spreading through her entire body, and she fleetingly found herself wondering who was supposed to be seducing who here.

'I'm sure we can come to some sort of mutual agreement.' Her voice came out as a sort of husky burr, more as a result of the sudden dryness of her throat than an attempt at sexiness. Still, it seemed to be working. Bodyguard man was still staring fixedly at her and, even if his granite expression hadn't softened, there was no doubt she was doing something right.

Raising her arms, Anna went to link them behind his neck. She had no clear thought of what she was doing except that maybe she could persuade him with flattery, or perhaps blackmail him after a kiss—he was certainly getting no more that—so that she could make her escape. It went against her feminist principles but desperate times called for desperate measures.

But before she had the chance to do anything of the sort this hateful man snatched at her wrists, easily clasping them in one hand and bringing them down to her chest at the same time as swinging his other arm around her waist to pull her snugly against him. Anna gasped, the contact with his body, *that* part of his body, the particular *swell* of that part of his body, ricocheting through her with clenching waves. Granite-faced he may be, but that wasn't the only part of his body she had managed to harden.

And, judging by the look on his face, her captor had been taken by surprise too. He was glaring at her with a mixture of horror and hunger, the hand clasping her wrists shaking very slightly before he tightened its grip. Controlling the tremble of her own body, Anna stared back. If this was a small victory, though small was hardly the right word, she was going to make the most of it. Tipping back her head, she trained her eyes on his, forcing his to meet them, to see the temptations that they held, temptations that burned so brightly, even if she had no intention of honouring them. She could sense the quickening of his heartbeat beneath his white shirt, hear the faint rasp in his exhaled breath. She had got him.

'Princess Anna!'

Suddenly there was a blinding flash of light, illuminating their bodies, freezing them against the backdrop of darkness.

'What the hell?' A low growl rumbled from Anna's captor as he spun around to face the photographer that had crept out of the shadows, the shutter of the camera clicking furiously.

Blinking against the glare, Anna felt her wrists being released as this warrior man lunged towards the photographer, clearly intent on murder. But when she went to move, to make her escape or save the photographer's life—she didn't know which—he was right back by her side again, pulling her forcefully into his arms.

'Oh, no, you don't. You're not going anywhere.'

'Come on, Anna. Show us a kiss!' Bolder now, the photographer took a step closer, the camera flashing all the time.

Anna had a split second to make a decision. If she wanted to get away from this man, avoid being frogmarched back to her own engagement party and forced to announce her betrothal to a man she could never, ever marry, there was one sure way to do it. Standing on tiptoes, she raised her arms to link them behind her captors head, shoving her fingers through the thick swathe of his hair and pulling against his resistance to bring him closer. If this was what the photographer wanted, this was what he was going to get.

With one final, terrifically brave or wildly foolish breath—Anna had no idea which—she reached up to plant her lips firmly on his.

What the hell?

Shock sucked the air from Zahir Zahani's lungs, numbing his senses, closing his fists. Plump and firm, her lips had swiftly turned from cold to warm as they sealed his own, the pressure increasing as she raked her hands through his hair to pull him closer. Her breath rasped between them, her delicate scent filling his nostrils, temporarily freezing his brain yet heating every other part of his body. Zahir went rigid, and the arms that were supposed to be restraining her were no more than useless weights as Annalina continued her relentless assault on his mouth. With the blood roaring in his ears, he found his lips parting, his body screaming to show her just where this could lead if she carried on this very dangerous game.

'Fantastic! Cheers for that, Anna.'

The camera flashes stopped and Annalina finally released him, letting her arms fall by her side. Meanwhile the photographer was already on his scooter, his camera slung over his shoulder.

'I owe you one!'

Turning the scooter around, he noisily zoomed off into the Paris streets, giving a cheery wave over his shoulder.

Zahir stared after him, suffering a split second of silent horror before his brain finally kicked into action again. Reaching into his jacket pocket, he grabbed his mobile phone. He'd have been able to catch the low life on foot if he didn't have this vixen to deal with. But his security team would pick him up—get him stopped and get the camera tossed into the Seine, the photographer along with it, if he had any say.

'No.' Her cold, trembling fingers closed over the phone in his hand. 'It's too late. It's done.'

'The hell it is.' Shaking off her hand, he started to punch in numbers. 'I can get him stopped. I *will* get him stopped.'

'There's no point.'

He stopped short, the cold determination in her voice halting his hand. 'And what exactly do you mean by that?' A trickle of dread started to seep into his veins.

'I'm sorry.' Dark-blue eyes shone back at him. 'But I had to do it.'

Hell! Realisation smacked him across the head. He'd been had. The whole thing was a set-up. This deceitful, conniving little princess had set a trap and he had walked right in. Fury coursed through him. He had no idea what her motive was but he did know that she would live to regret it. *Nobody* made a fool of Zahir Zahani.

'You will be sorry, believe me.' He kept his voice deliberately low, concentrating on controlling the rage that was pumping adrenaline dangerously fast around his veins. 'You will be more than sorry for what you have done.'

'I had no choice!' Her voice was full of anguish now and she even reached out a trembling hand to touch his arm before demurely lowering her eyes to the ground.

Nice try, Princess. But you don't get to fool me more than once.

Roughly grasping her chin, Zahir tipped back her head so she couldn't escape his searing gaze. He wanted her to look at him. He wanted her to know exactly who she was dealing with here.

'Oh, you had a choice, all right. You've chosen to bring scandal and disrepute to both our countries. And, trust me, you are going to pay for that, young lady. But first you are going to tell me why.'

He saw her slender body begin to tremble, her bare shoulders hunch against the shiver that ran through her. Bizarrely he itched to touch her, to warm that tantalisingly goose-bumped skin with his hot hands. But he would do no such thing.

'Because I am desperate.' Clear blue eyes implored him.

'Desperate?' He repeated the word with disgust.

'Yes. I can't go back to that party.'

'So that's why you set up this little charade?'

'No, I didn't set it up, not in the way you mean. I just took advantage of the situation.' Her voice lowered.

'You tricked me into following you. You arranged for that photographer to be there.'

'No! I had no idea that either of you had followed me.'

'You're lying. That guy knew you.'

'He didn't know me. He knows who I am. There's a difference. The press have been following me around all my life.'

'So you are telling me this wasn't planned?'

Annalina shook her head.

'Think carefully before you speak, Princess. Because, I have to warn you, to lie to me now would be very foolish indeed.'

'It was a spur-of-the-moment decision. And that is the truth.'

Despite everything, Zahir found himself believing her. He dragged in a breath. 'So that… that little display you just put on…?' He curled his lip against the traitorous memory of the way she had leant into him, the way she had messed with his head. 'What exactly did you hope to achieve? What makes you so desperate that you would bring disgrace upon your family? Fabricate a scandal to rock the foundations of both of our countries?'

'Disgrace I can live with. I'm used to it.' Her voice was suddenly very small. 'And the scandal will die down. But to be forced to marry Rashid Zahani is more than I can bear. That would have been a life sentence.'

'How dare you disrespect the King in this way?' Defensive anger roared in his voice. 'The engagement will still be announced. The marriage will still go ahead.'

'No. You can force me to go back to the party, even force me, with the help of my father, to go ahead with the announcement of the engagement. But, once those photographs go online, I'll be dropped like a stone.'

Zahir stared into the beautiful face of this wilful princess. Her skin was so pale in this ghostly light, so delicate, it was almost translucent. But her lips were ruby-red and her eyes as blue as the evening sky.

He knew with a leaden certainty that she meant what she said. There was no way she was going to go through with this marriage. He could still find that photographer, destroy the photos, but ultimately what good would it do? What was to be gained?

Hell and damnation. After all the planning that had gone into this union, the careful handling, the wretched party… It had taken all his powers of persuasion to get Rashid to agree to marry this European princess at all. Months of negotiations to get to this point. And for what? To have the whole thing thrown back in their faces and Rashid humiliated in the most degrading way. No, he could not let that happen. He *would* not let that happen. He had been a fool to trust this wayward princess, to believe the empty promises of her desperate father. But the situation had gone too far now—he had to try and salvage something from this mess. He had to come up with a clever solution.

Decision made, he took hold of Annalina's arm.

'You will accompany me back to the party and we will seek out the King and tell him what has happened. Then we will announce your engagement.'

'Didn't you understand a word I said?' The fight was back in her eyes. 'The King won't marry me now. That's the reason I just did what I did.'

'We will announce your engagement—not to the King, but to his brother, the Prince.'

'Yeah, great idea! I take it you must be employed more for your brawn than your brains.' Zahir felt every muscle in his body stiffen at her mocking jibe. He was going to enjoy punishing her for her insolence. 'The Prince is hardly going to want to marry me either, is he?'

'As of five minutes ago, the Prince has no choice.'

Narrowing his eyes, Zahir watched defiance turn to confusion turn to a creeping realisation. A strangely perverse sense of pleasure stole over him.

Her trembling hand flew to her mouth then

made a fist as she stuffed it between her lips, biting down onto her knuckles to stifle her cry.

'Ah, yes, Princess, I see the truth is dawning.' Zahir threw back his shoulders, almost enjoying himself. 'I am Zahir Zahani, Prince of Nabatean, brother of King Rashid. And, as of five minutes ago, your future husband.'

CHAPTER TWO

ANNA FELT FOR the railings of the bridge behind her, grabbing at the bars to stop herself from sliding to the ground.

'You...you are Prince Zahir?'

One arrogant, scowling dark brow raised fractionally in reply.

No. It wasn't possible. The full horror of what she had done gnawed away at her brain. Being caught in a clinch with a bodyguard to get out of her engagement was one thing, but for the 'bodyguard' to be the fiancé's brother was quite another. This went far beyond the realms of scandal. This could cause an international incident.

'I... I had no idea.'

He shrugged. 'Evidently.'

'We need to do something—quickly.' Panic caught up with her, squeezing her vocal cords, spinning her brain around in her head. 'We must stop that photographer.'

Still Zahir Zahani didn't move. What was wrong with him? Why wasn't he doing anything? Anna felt as if she were in a terrible dream, running and running but getting no further away from the monster.

Finally he spoke. 'To use your phrase, Princess, *it's too late. It's done.*'

'But that was before I knew… There's still time to find him, pay him off, stop him.'

'Possibly. But I have no intention of doing any such thing.'

'Wh…what do you mean?' Confusion and frustration held her in their grip, hysteria not far behind. 'I don't understand.'

'Because, like you, I intend to take advantage of the situation. We will go back to the party and we will announce our engagement. Just as I said.'

Horror now joined the bedlam in her head. He wasn't serious. Surely he didn't mean it? She stared into his cold, forbidding features. *Oh, God.* He did—he really did!

Releasing the railings, she pushed herself upright, immediately dwarfed by this towering figure of a man who was blocking her way, her vision, her ability to think clearly. 'No! We can't. The idea is preposterous.'

'Is it, Princess Annalina? He glowered down at her. 'How will you feel tomorrow when those photographs are published? When you have to face your father, your people and the rest of the world? Are you prepared for the consequences?'

Her face crumpled.

'As I thought.' His mocking voice echoed in the dark around them. 'Not quite so preposterous now, is it? You have no alternative but to do as I say.'

'No. There has to be another way.' *Think, Anna, think.* Why did her poor brain seem to have turned to sludge? 'If the photographs are published I'll simply explain that it was all a misunderstanding—that I didn't know who you were…that it meant nothing.'

'And that would achieve what, exactly? Apart from prove that you are the sort of tramp who goes around seducing total strangers on the eve of your engagement and that your fiancé's own brother was caught in your trap. I would never subject Rashid to such humiliation.'

There was a second of silence.

'But we can't just swap!'

'We can and we will. The arrangements are all in place. A commitment has been made between our two countries—between your father and the Kingdom of Nabatean. He has offered your hand and it has been accepted. Nothing will stand in the way of that.' His shadowed face was as hard as stone. 'The commitment will be honoured.'

'But the commitment was to your brother—not you.'

'Then perhaps you should have thought of that before you ran away and started this whole debacle, betraying the trust my brother had put in you.' Anna lowered her eyes against the force of his biting scorn. 'Fortunately for you, it makes no difference which brother honours the commitment. The same objectives will be achieved either way.'

'And that's it? Honouring the commitment is all that matters to you?' She thrashed about, trying to find a way out. 'How can you be so unemotional? This is a marriage we are talking about, a bond that has to last a lifetime.'

'Don't you think I know that, Princess?' Lowering his head, Zahir hissed into her ear, sending a bolt of electricity through her. 'Don't you think I am fully aware of the sacrifice I am making? But, if it is emotion you are looking for, I must warn you to be careful. To expose my opinion of you would be straying into a dark and dangerous territory indeed.'

Cloaked in menace, his words settled over her like a shroud. Anna bit down hard on her lip to control the shiver. She didn't entirely know what he meant by that chilling statement. She wasn't sure she wanted to.

'And if I refuse?' Still she tried, squirming like a worm on a fish hook.

'All I can say is, to refuse would be extremely stupid.' He paused, weighting his words with care. 'I'm sure I don't have to remind you that you already have one failed engagement behind you. Another might cause considerable speculation.'

A sharp jab of pain went through her. So he knew about that, did he? About her humiliating broken engagement to Prince Henrik. Of course he did. Everyone did.

Tears were starting to build now, blocking her throat, scratching at her eyes. Tears of frustration, self-pity and wretched misery that her life had come to this. That she should be forced to marry a man who clearly despised her. A man who was as terrifying as he was alien—an arrogant, untamed brute of a man the like of which she had never come across before. She hadn't begun to process the extraordinary reaction between them when she'd kissed him, the shockingly carnal way his body had responded. That would have to be for another time. But she did know he would never make her happy—that was a certainty. He would never even try.

'You have brought this upon yourself, Princess Annalina.' Somewhere outside the buzz of her head she heard him relentlessly press home the point. 'You have forced my hand, but I am prepared do my duty. And, ultimately, so must you.'

His damning statement was the final nail in the coffin.

And so it was that Anna found herself being unceremoniously marched back to the hotel to meet her fate. With Zahir's arm around her waist, propelling her forward, she had had no choice but to stumble along beside him, needing two or three stiletto-heeled steps to match his forceful stride as he rapidly navigated them through the Parisian streets. Her heart was thumping wildly, her dry breath scouring her throat as she tried to come to terms with what she was about to do—tie herself to this man for ever. But with the heat of his arm burning through the sheer fabric of her dress she found herself trying to fight that assault, the whole shimmering force of his nearness, his muscled flesh, his masculine scent, leaving her brain no space to cope with anything else.

Finally outside the hotel Zahir turned her around to face him, his gaze raking mercilessly over her pale face. With the light spilling from the hotel, they could see each other more clearly now, but Anna had to tear her eyes away from his cruelly handsome features, afraid of what she might see there. Her gaze slid down the broad column of his neck to the open buttons of his shirt, the grey silk tie tugged to one side. And there, plainly visible against the exposed olive skin, was the livid red mark—the bite, where she had sunk her teeth into him. Instinctively her hand flew to her chest.

Alerted by her stare, Zahir swiftly moved to do up his shirt and straighten his tie, his knowing glare spelling out exactly what he thought of her barbarism.

'We will go in together,' he began coldly. 'You will talk to our guests and behave in the appropriate manner. But say nothing to anyone about the engagement. I will find my brother and tell him of the new arrangement.'

Anna nodded, swallowing down her dread. 'But shouldn't I be there when you speak to your brother? Don't I owe him that?'

'I think it's a little late for the guilt to kick in now, Annalina. We are way past that. *I* will deal with Rashid and then explain the situation to your father. Only then can we announce our engagement.'

Her father. In her frenzied state Anna had almost forgotten the man who had brought about this hideous debacle in the first place. It had been King Gustav who had insisted that his only child should marry King Rashid of Nabatean, leaving her no room to argue. Not after she had already let him down once, let her country down, by failing to secure a successful match between herself and Prince Henrik of Ebsberg—something that still both humiliated and swamped Anna with relief in equal measure.

A cold, heartless man, King Gustav had never recovered from the death of his wife, Annalina's mother, who had suffered a fatal brain aneurysm when Anna had been just seven years old. The shock had been too much for him and it seemed to Anna that a part of her father had died with her mother. The loving, caring part. It seemed that just when she had needed him most he had turned away from her. And had never turned back.

He would be utterly furious to find out that she had messed up again—that she was refusing to marry Rashid Zahani and was chucking away the chance to provide financial stability for Dorrada. At least, he would have been, if she hadn't had an alternative plan to offer him. For the first time Anna felt a tinge of relief about what she was doing. Zahir might be the second son but everything about him suggested power and authority, far more so than his elder brother, in fact. She suspected that her father would have no problem accepting the new arrangement. Somehow she had to find it inside herself to do the same.

She looked down, concentrating on arranging the folds of her dress, all too aware of the fire in Zahir's eyes as they licked over her, missing nothing.

'You are ready?'

She nodded, not trusting herself to speak.

'Very well, then, we will do this.'

The arm snaked around her waist again and together they ascended the red-carpeted steps, the hotel doorman ushering them in with a polite bow.

The scene inside the ballroom appeared even more daunting than when Anna had fled less than an hour ago. More people had arrived, swelling the numbers into the hundreds, and they were milling around beneath the magnificent domed ceiling of the gilded room, illuminated by dozens of huge chandeliers and watched from above by carved marble statues. The air of anticipation had increased too. Anyone who was anyone was here, the great and the good from a host of European and Middle Eastern countries gathered at the invitation of King Gustav of Dorrada for a celebration that had yet to be disclosed.

Not that it took much working out. Presumably everyone in the room knew what this party was in aid of—or at least thought they did. It was common knowledge that King Gustav had been trying, and failing, to make a good marriage for his only daughter for some time. And the newly formed kingdom of Nabatean desperately needed entrée into the notoriously closed shop of 'old' Europe. The fact that the party was being held here, in one of the oldest and most exclusive hotels in Paris, right at the heart of Europe, bore testament to that and was certainly no coincidence.

Anna looked around her, the heat and the noise thundering inside her head, shredding her nerves, fuelling her panic. Zahir had left her side and gone in search of his brother, which should have been a relief, but bizarrely only made her feel more vulnerable and exposed. She could see her father in the distance and her heart took up a shaky beat at the thought of what he was about to be told. Of what they were about to do.

Grabbing a glass of champagne from a passing waiter, she took a deep gulp, followed by a deep breath, and, pulling on what she hoped was the suitably starry-eyed expression of a fiancée-to-be, set about mingling with her guests.

It was not long before Zahir was by her side again. Taking her arm, he steered her away from the curious stares of the small group of people she had been trying to converse with, guests who were clearly starting to wonder what was going on. Anna didn't know who else had witnessed it, but a few minutes ago she had caught sight of Rashid skirting around the edge of the room. Their eyes had met for a fleeting second before he had lowered his head and hurried from the ballroom.

'The necessary arrangements have been made.' Zahir's voice was steely with determination. 'It's time for the announcement.'

So this was it, then. Part of her thought she might wake up at any moment, that this was some sort of crazy dream—no, correction, nightmare. But as she slipped her arm through his, felt herself being pulled to his side, her whole body lit up to his nearness. Her heart thumped as the smooth fabric of his dinner jacket brushed against her bare arm, pinpricks of awareness skittering across her skin. This was real all right. This was actually happening.

As they moved across the floor of the ballroom the guests parted to let them through, something about the purposefulness of Zahir's stride or maybe the mask-like expression on Annalina's face, halting their conversations as they turned to look at them, curiosity glinting in their eyes.

Silencing the orchestra with a raised hand, Zahir waited a second for complete quiet to descend before he began.

'I would like to thank everyone for coming this evening.'

Anna heard his calm words through the roaring of her ears. She could feel hundreds of pairs of eyes trained on her.

'We are here to celebrate the coming together of two great nations—Dorrada and the Kingdom of Nabatean. Our countries are to be joined together by the age-old tradition of matrimony.' He paused, scanning the room, which had gone deathly quiet. 'I would like to formally announce that Princess Annalina and I are to be married.'

There was a collective gasp of surprise, followed by furtive whisperings. Obviously Princess Annalina was not marrying the brother the guests had been expecting. Then a small cheer went up and people started to applaud, calling out their congratulations.

Anna's father appeared by her side and she felt for his hand, the little girl in her suddenly needing his reassurance. The smallest squeeze of encouragement would have done. Anything to show that he was pleased with her. That he loved her. He leant towards her and for one hopeful moment Anna thought he was going to do just that, but all hopes were dashed when he whispered in her ear, 'Don't you dare let me down again, Annalina.' Extricating his hand, he took a glass of champagne from the proffered silver tray and waited for Anna and Zahir to do the same. Then, refusing to meet his daughter's eye, he cleared his throat and proposed a toast, instructing everyone to raise their glasses to the happy couple and the future prosperity of their joined nations.

Anna gripped the stem of her glass as their names were chorused by the guests. Beside her she could sense Zahir, all rigid authority and unyielding control, while the false smile she had plastered across her face was in danger of cracking at any moment. In terms of appearing to be a happy couple, she doubted they were fooling anyone. But that wasn't what this was about, was it? This betrothal was a straightforward business deal. Anna just wished that someone would tell her stupid heart.

The next hour was a torturous round of introductions and small talk as Zahir swept her around the room, making sure she was welded to his side at all times. He moved between the ministers and ambassadors of Nabatean, the diplomats and high-ranking officials of Dorrada. It was blatantly nothing more than a networking exercise, making contact with the people that mattered. Congratulations were swiftly swept aside in favour of discussions about policies and politics, Anna left smiling inanely at the wives of these important men, and forced to display the stunning ring on her finger for them to coo over yet again.

Finally finding themselves at the entrance to the ballroom, Zahir announced in lowered tones that they had done their duty and it would now be acceptable for them to leave.

Anna gave a sigh of relief but, looking up, she was immediately caught in the midnight black of Zahir's hooded gaze. Suddenly she felt awkward, like a teenager on her first date. 'I will say goodnight, then.' She went to turn away, desperate to escape to her hotel room, to be free of her captor, at least for a few hours. More than anything she wanted to be alone, to have time to try to come to terms with what she had done.

'Not so fast.' With lightning speed, Zahir laid a restraining hold on her arm. 'This day has not ended yet.'

Anna's heart skipped a beat. What did he mean by that? Surely he wasn't expecting…? He didn't think…? Heat flared across her cheeks, spreading down her neck to her chest that heaved beneath its tight-fitting bodice. Somewhere deep inside her a curl of lust unfurled.

'I can assure you that it has, Zahir.' She touched primly at her hair. 'I don't know what you are suggesting, but for your information I intend to go to bed now—alone.'

'You flatter yourself, young lady.' Scorn leeched from his voice. 'For your information, I do not intend to make any claims on your body.' He paused, eyes flashing with lethal intent. 'Not tonight, at least. But neither will I be letting you out of my sight. Not yet. Not until I feel I can trust you.'

'What do you mean?' Desperately trying to claw back some composure, she folded her arms across her chest. 'You can hardly keep me prisoner until our marriage.' Even as she said the words the terrible thought struck her that maybe he could. He was a man of such power, such authority, it was as if his very being demanded to be obeyed. The glittering lights of the ballroom had only accentuated his might, his towering height, the long legs and the broad, muscled shoulders that refused to be tamed by the fine material of his dinner jacket. Anna had noticed several women openly staring at him, their refined good manners deserting them in the face of this ruggedly handsome man.

'Not a prisoner, Princess. But let's just say I want to keep you somewhere that I can see you.'

'But that is ridiculous. I have given you my

word, made the promise to my father. We have announced our engagement to the world. What more do I have to do to convince you?'

'You have to earn my trust, Annalina.' His eyes roamed over her, flat and considering. 'And that, as I'm sure you won't be surprised to hear, may take some time.'

'So what are you saying?' Anna bristled beneath his harsh scrutiny. 'That until I've earned this so-called trust you're not going to let me out of your sight? That hardly seems practical. Not least because we happen to live on different continents.'

Zahir shrugged. 'That is of little consequence. The solution is simple—you will return with me to Nabatean.'

Anna stared back at him. His knowing gaze was doing strange things to her head—making it swim. She must have drunk too much champagne.

'That's right, Princess Annalina.' Cold and authoritative, he confirmed what she feared. 'We leave tonight.'

CHAPTER THREE

ANNA PEERED OUT of the window as the plane started to descend, the sight of the dawn sky making her catch her breath. Below her shimmered Medira, the capital city of Nabatean, glowing in the pinks and golds of a new day. Her first glimpse of the country that would be her new home was certainly a stunning one. But it did nothing to lighten Anna's heart.

The little she knew about Nabatean had been gleaned during the first panicked days after she had been informed that she was to marry King Rashid Zahani. There had been a bloody civil war—that much she did know—when the people of Nabatean had fought bravely to overthrow the oppressive regime of Uristan, eventually winning independence and becoming a country in its own right again after more than fifty years.

There had been mention of Rashid and Zahir's parents, the former King and Queen of

Nabatean, who had returned after living in exile, only to be murdered by rebel insurgents on the eve of the country's independence. Details of the horrifically tragic event were few and far between and in part Anna was grateful for that. There was frustratingly little documented about the new country at all and she realised just how ignorant she was about the place that she would somehow have to learn to call home.

Just as she knew so little of the man who was bringing her here, who intended to make her his wife. The man who had taken himself off to the office area of the luxury private jet and had spent the long journey so immersed in work, either glued to his laptop or reading through documents, that he had paid her no attention at all.

But what did she expect? When they had boarded the jet he had suggested that Anna retire to the bedroom, making it quite clear that the space would be her own. But stubbornness, or the fact that she knew she would never be able to sleep, or the hope that they might be able to have some meaningful discussion, had made her decline his offer.

Now she knew just how futile that hope had been and, staring at her own anxious reflection in the glass, found herself wondering how it was that her life had always been so controlled by others. First her father and now this dark, brooding force of nature that was to be her husband. Her destiny had never been her own. And now it never would be.

'We land in ten minutes.' With a start, Anna turned around to see that Zahir was standing right beside her, his hand on the back of her seat. For such a large man he moved surprisingly quietly, stealthily. Even his voice was different—raw and untamed, as if capable of sinful pleasure or brutal destruction. 'The distance from the airport to the palace is not a long one. Your journey is almost over. I trust you haven't found it too arduous?'

'No, I'm fine.' That was a lie. She was totally exhausted. But, having turned down his offer of an in-flight bedroom, she wasn't going to admit that.

'I think you will find the palace is most comfortable. You can rest assured that your every need will be catered for.'

'Thanks.' Anna didn't know what else to say. Who did he think she was? A princess from a fairy tale who would be unable to sleep should a pea be placed under her mattress? Or, worse still, some sort of prima donna who expected her every whim instantly to be obeyed?

If so, he couldn't be more wrong. She might

have been raised in a palace but it had been as echoing and draughty as it was ancient, with crumbling walls, peeling paintwork and plumbing that only worked when it felt like it. And, as for expecting her every need to be catered for, well, she had been brought up to have no needs, no special treatment. Since her mother's death a succession of nannies—each one more severe, more cold-hearted than the last—had been at pains to point that out to her. Whether it was because they'd been handpicked by her father for that very reason—King Gustav believed his daughter needed a firm hand—or because the chilly conditions of the palace somehow had rubbed off on them, Anna didn't know.

She did know that she had never found anyone who had been able to replicate the warm feeling of her mother's arms around her, or the soft cushion of her breast, or the light touch of her fingers as she'd swept Annalina's unruly hair from her eyes. Which was why she held on to those feelings as firmly as her seven-year-old's grip would allow, keeping them alive by remembering everything she could about her beloved mother, refusing to let the memories fade.

A fleet of limousines was there to whisk Zahir and Anna, plus Rashid and assorted members of staff who had accompanied them on the plane, on the final leg of their journey to the palace. Once inside the palace, they were greeted by more deferential staff and Anna was shown to her suite of rooms, the bedroom dominated by an enormous gilded bed that was surmounted by a coronet and swathes of luxurious, deep-red silk.

It looked incredibly inviting. Finally giving way to her tiredness, Anna headed for the bathroom for a quick shower, taking in the huge, sunken marble bath with its flashy gold fittings and the veined marble walls. Then, climbing into the bed, she closed her eyes and let herself sink into deep, dream-filled sleep.

She was awoken by a tap on the door. Two dark-haired young women appeared, each bearing a tray laden with fruit, cheese, eggs, hummus, pitta bread and olives. She sat forward as they silently plumped up the pillows behind her, then one started to pour a cup of coffee whilst the other one held a plate and a pair of tongs, presumably waiting for Anna to make her selection.

'Oh, thank you.' Pushing the hair out of her eyes, Anna smiled at them, wondering how on earth she was ever going to do justice to this feast. What time was it anyway? A gilded clock on the wall opposite showed it to be just past one o'clock. So, that would be one in the afternoon? She looked back at the food. She was going to have to choose something. Judging by the earnest look on the young girls' faces, she wouldn't have been surprised if they had offered to feed her themselves. 'I think I'll try the eggs—they look delicious.'

Immediately an omelette was set before her and two pairs of eyes watched as she tentatively dug in her fork.

'Do you speak English?' Anna took a mouthful of omelette followed by a mouthful of coffee. The latter was strong, dark and utterly delicious.

'Yes, Your Highness.'

'Does everyone in Nabatean speak English?'

'Yes, Your Highness, it is our second language. You will find everyone can speak it.'

'It's the second language in my country too, so that's handy.' Anna smiled at these two pretty young women. 'And please, call me Annalina. "Your Highness" sounds far too stuffy.'

The women nodded but something told Anna that they would struggle with such informality. 'Can I ask your names?'

'I am Lena and this is Layla.'

'What pretty names. I'm guessing you are sisters?' She tried another forkful of omelette.

'We are. Layla is my younger sister by two years.'

'Well, it's very nice to meet you. Have you worked here in the palace long?' If she couldn't manage to eat much, at least she could distract them with conversation.

'Yes, for nearly two years. Ever since the palace was built. We are very lucky. After our parents died we were given a home in return for serving the King and Prince Zahir.'

So their parents were dead. Anna suspected there were going to be many tales of death and destruction in this country once ravaged by war. She wanted to ask more but Lena's lowered eyes suggested to pry further would be insensitive. Layla, however, had edged closer to the bed, staring at her as if she had been dropped down from another planet.

'I like your hair.'

'Layla!' Her sister admonished her with a sharp rebuke.

'That's okay.' Anna laughed, looking down at the blonde locks that were tumbling in disarray over her shoulders. 'Thank you for the compliment. It takes a lot of brushing in the morning, though, to get the tangles out.'

'I can do that for you,' Layla replied earnestly.

'Well, that's very kind of you but…'

'We are honoured to be able to serve you, Your Royal Highness,' Lena said. 'Prince Zahir has instructed us to attend to your every need.'

He had? Anna found it hard to believe that he would concern himself with such trivialities as her every need. 'Well, in that case, I will take you up on your kind offer. Prince Zahir...' Anna hesitated. She wanted to ask what sort of an employer he was, what sort of a man they thought he was, but suspected that they wouldn't be at liberty to tell her and it would be unfair to ask. 'Do you see very much of him?'

'No. He is away from the palace a lot. And, even when he is here, his needs are very few.'

'Do you have many visitors, here in the palace?'

'Not so many. Mostly foreign businessmen and politicians.'

'We've never had a visitor as pretty as you before,' Layla offered conversationally. 'Do all the women in your country look like you?'

'Well, the women of Dorrada tend to be fair-skinned and blue-eyed. The men too, come to that. Your dark beauty would be much prized in my country. As I'm sure it is here.'

'So, Prince Zahir...' Layla continued. 'You think him handsome?'

'Layla!'

'I am only asking.' Layla stuck out her bottom lip.

'Obviously she thinks him handsome. She wouldn't be marrying him otherwise.'

Anna suppressed a smile as the two sisters set about one another in their own language, waiting for them to finish before speaking again.

'The answer to your question is yes—I do think him handsome.'

The sisters exchanged an excited glance.

'And it is true that you will be marrying and coming to live here in the palace?' This time Lena asked the question, her curiosity overcoming her sense of decorum.

'Yes, that is true.' Saying it out loud didn't make it seem any the less astonishing.

Lena's and Layla's pretty faces broke out into broad smiles and they even reached to clasp each other's hands.

'That is very good news, Your Royal Highness. Very good news indeed.'

Staring at the screen, Zahir cursed under his breath. He had braced himself for a small photograph of the two of them on the bridge, prepared to suffer the mild humiliation of being caught kissing in public, or rather being kissed, when it was put in the wider context of the engagement party. But this wasn't a small photograph. This was a series of images, blown up to reveal every minor detail. With his finger jabbing on the mouse, Zahir scrolled down and down, his blood pressure rocketing as more and more pictures of him locked in a passionate embrace with Annalina flashed before his eyes. There were even several close-ups of the engagement ring, worn on the slender hand that was threaded through his hair, before finally the official photographs of the party appeared, the ones he wanted the world to see. The ones where he and Annalina were standing solemnly side by side, displaying their commitment to each other and to their countries.

And it wasn't just one newspaper. The whole of Europe appeared to be obsessed with the beautiful Princess Annalina, the press in France, the UK, and of course Dorrada itself taking a particular interest, feasting on the titbits that the photographer had no doubt sold to them for a handsome fee.

A rustle behind him made him turn his head and there stood the object of the press's attention, Annalina. At last—it was over an hour since he had sent servants to her room to find out what she was doing, giving orders that she should meet him here in the stateroom at her earliest convenience. Clearly he was going to have to be more specific. Dressed in a simple navy fitted dress, she looked both young, chic and incredibly sexy at the same time. Her ash-blonde hair was loose, tumbling over her shoulders in soft waves, falling well below the swell of her breasts.

Zahir felt his throat go dry. He hadn't been prepared for such hair, only having seen it secured on top of her head in some way before. He had had no idea it would be so long, so fascinating. He had had no idea that he would be fighting the urge to imagine how it would feel against his bare skin.

'Have you seen this?' Angry with himself, with his reaction and this whole damned situation, his voice rasped harshly. He hadn't been able to concentrate all morning, hadn't got through half the work he'd intended to.

She glanced at the laptop, screwing up her eyes. 'Is it bad?'

'See for yourself.'

A soft cloud of floral scent washed over him as she sat down next to him, tucking her hair behind one small, perfect ear. He almost flinched as she reached across him to touch the mouse, quickly scrolling through the images and scanning the text as she moved from one website to the next.

'Well.' She turned in her seat to look at him, her eyes a startling blue. 'I guess it's no worse than we were expecting.'

'You, maybe. I certainly wasn't expecting such mass coverage.'

'Well, there's nothing we can do about it now.' She exhaled, the light breath whispering across the bare skin of his forearm and raising the hairs, raising his blood pressure. 'Are the photos in the Nabatean newspapers too?'

'Fortunately not. The official photographs from the engagement party are all that they will see. My people would not be interested in such a sordid spectacle.'

He watched as she wrinkled her small nose. Her skin was so pale, so clear, like the finest porcelain.

'What?' He didn't want to ask, he hadn't even meant to ask. But her disrespectful gesture refused to be ignored.

'I'm just wondering how you know that—if they aren't given the chance, I mean. That sounds like censorship to me.'

Temper snaked through him, slowing his heart to a dull thud. He narrowed his eyes, the thick lashes blurring his image of this infuriating woman. 'Let me make something clear right from the start, Princess Annalina. I may, or may not, seek your views on matters to do with European culture and traditions that I am not familiar with. That is your role. However, you do *not* attempt to interfere with the running of my country. Your opinions are neither needed nor wanted.'

'If you say so.'

'I do.'

'All I'm saying is…' she raised finely shaped eyebrows '…you can't have it both ways.' It seemed she was determined to stand up to him. To have the last word. 'If you are marrying me solely because I am a Western princess, because you want entrée into Europe that my family, my country, can give you, then you are going to have to accept this sort of media attention. It comes with the job. It comes with me.'

Zahir scowled. Was this true? If so he was going to have to put a stop to it. He had no intention of becoming part of some celebrity circus. But then twenty-four hours ago he had had no intention of marrying at all.

'I have to say, I am somewhat surprised that you would be happy for the first sighting the people of Nabatean have of their new princess to be a grubby little paparazzi shot of you wantonly pressing your body up against mine.' He wished he hadn't reminded himself of that now. Not when she was so close. Not when he knew he wanted her to do it again.

'It doesn't bother me.' She tossed her head, her hair rippling over her shoulders, deliberately countering his pomposity with a throwaway remark. It felt to Zahir as if she was throwing his weakness for her back in his face too, even though he had gone to great pains to cover it up.

'Well, it should bother you. It is hardly becoming.' The pomposity solidified inside him, holding him ramrod-straight.

'Look. The paparazzi have been following me all my life. I'm used to it—it's part of the role I was unwittingly born into. There are probably hundreds of images of me being *unbecoming*, as you put it.'

Zahir felt himself pale beneath his olive skin. This was worse than he'd thought. In his haste to arrange a suitable match for his brother it appeared he hadn't been thorough enough in his research. He knew there had been a broken engagement but what was she telling him now? That she had a history of debauched behaviour? This woman who he now had to take as his wife.

'It's okay!' Suddenly she let out a laugh, a light-hearted chuckle that echoed between them, seeming to surprise the cavernous room as much as it did him. 'There's no need to look like that.' Now she was reaching for his hand, laying her own over the top of it. 'I haven't done anything really terrible! And, who knows, maybe now that I'm officially engaged the paparazzi will lose interest in me, find someone else to train their zoom lenses on. Especially as you are not well known in Europe.'

'Unlike your last fiancé, you mean?'

Annalina withdrew her hand, all traces of humour gone now, colour touching her cheeks at his mention of her former partner. If he had wanted to snuff out her sunshine, he had achieved it.

'Well, yes, Prince Henrik was well known to the gossip columnists. When that relationship ended it was inevitable that there was going to be a feeding frenzy.'

There was silence as Zahir refilled his coffee cup before returning his gaze to Annalina's face.

'I expect you want to know what happened.' She twisted her hands in her lap.

'No.'

'I will tell you if you ask.'

'I have no intention of asking. It's none of my business.' And, more than that, he didn't want to think about it. She continued to stare at him, a strange sort of expression playing across her face, as if she was trying to decide where to go from here.

'I suggest we concentrate on making plans for the future.' There, he could be sensitive, moving her on from what was obviously a painful subject.

'Yes, of course.'

'I see no reason for a long engagement.'

'No.' Now she was chewing her lip.

'A month should be ample time to make the arrangements. I'm assuming you'll want some sort of society wedding in Dorrada? If we follow that with a blessing here in Nabatean, that should suffice.'

'Right.'

'So I can leave you to organise it? The wedding, I mean? Or hire people to do it, or however these things work.' At the mention of the wedding she seemed to have gone into some kind of stupor. Wasn't the idea of arranging your wedding day supposed to be appealing to a young woman? Clearly not to Annalina. A thought occurred to him and he leant back in his chair. 'If it's money that is concerning you, let me assure you that is not a problem. No expense is to be spared.'

But instead of lessening her worry his statement only furrowed her brow deeper and was now coupled with a distinct look of distaste in her eyes. Perhaps talking about money was distasteful—he had no idea, and frankly he didn't care. Or perhaps he was the thing that she found distasteful. He didn't want to care about that either. But somehow he did. Abruptly scraping back his chair, he pushed himself to his feet, suddenly needing to end this meeting right now.

'Perhaps you will inform me of the date of the wedding as soon as you know it.'

He looked down on Annalina from the superior position of his height. He heard himself, cold and aloof.

CHAPTER FOUR

'YOUR ROYAL HIGHNESS?'

Anna was wandering around the palace when one of the servants came to find her. She had spent the last hour pacing from one room to the next, still fuming too much over Zahir's abrupt departure from their so-called meeting to pay much attention to her opulent surroundings. The way he had just got up and walked out, ending their discussion with no warning, no manners!

She had thought she would try and distract herself by finding her way around this grand edifice but it was all too huge, too daunting, each room grander than the last, all domed ceilings, brightly coloured marble floors and micro-mosaic decorations. But there was nothing homely about it. In fact it had a new, unlived-in feel to it, as if no laughter had ever echoed through its stately rooms, no children's feet had ever raced along its miles of corridors or young bottoms slid down its sweepingly ornate banisters. Which, no doubt, they hadn't. This was a show home, nothing more. A monument erected as a display of wealth and power, a symbol of national pride for the people of Nabatean.

'Prince Zahir has instructed that you are to meet him at the palace entrance.' The servant bowed respectfully. 'If you would like to follow me?'

So that would be right now, would it? This was how it was to be—Zahir issued his orders and she was expected to obey. Just like any other member of his staff. Instinctively Anna wanted to rebel, to say no, just to prove that she wasn't at his beck and call. But what would that achieve, other than deliberately antagonising him? Something which she strongly suspected would not prove to be a good idea. Besides, she had nothing else to do.

A wall of heat hit her when she stepped out into the searing afternoon sun. Shielding her eyes, she could see Zahir standing by the limousine, waiting for the chauffeur to help her inside before getting in beside her.

'Can I ask where we're going?' She settled in her seat, preparing herself to turn and look at him. It still gave her a jolt every single time her eyes met his, every time she stared into his darkly rugged features. It was like a cattle prod to her nervous system. He had changed into a sharply cut suit, she noticed, so presumably this wasn't a pleasure trip.

'The Assembly House in the town square.' He returned her gaze. 'I have arranged a meeting with some officials, members of the senate and the government. It will be an opportunity to introduce you to them, so they can put a face to the name.'

A face to the name? His cold phrase left her in no doubt as to her role here—she was nothing more than a puppet, to be dangled in front of the people that mattered, jiggled around to perform when necessary and presumably put back in her box when she wasn't required. It was a depressing picture but she had to remember that this was what their union was all about, a mutually reciprocal arrangement for the benefit of both of their countries. Nothing more. She needed to catch her sinking stomach before it fell still further.

Breaking his gaze, Anna turned to look out of the window as the limousine swept them through the streets of Medira. It was a city still under construction, enormous cranes swinging above their heads, towering skyscrapers proudly rocketing heavenwards. The place certainly had a buzz about it. Lowering her head, Annalina peered up in awe.

'I hadn't realised Medira was such a metropolis. Is it really true that this whole city has been built in under two years?'

'It has, in common with several other major cities in Nabatean.'

'That's amazing. You must be very proud.'

'It has been a great responsibility.'

Responsibility. The word might as well be indelibly etched across his forehead. In fact it was, Anna realised as she turned to look at him again. It was there in the frown lines that crossed his brow, lines that furrowed into deep grooves when he was lost in thought or displeased. Which seemed to be most of the time. There was no doubt how heavily responsibility weighed on Zahir Zahani's shoulders, that his duty to his country knew no bounds. He was prepared to marry her, after all. What greater sacrifice was there than that?

'But you have achieved so much.' For some reason she wanted to ease his burden. 'Surely you must allow yourself a small acknowledgement of that?'

'The acknowledgement will come from the people, not me. They are the judge and jury. Everything we are doing here in Nabatean is for them.'

'Of course.' Anna turned to look out of the window again. It was pointless trying to reason with him. Through the shimmering heat she could now make out a mountain range, grey against the startling blue of the sky. She was used to mountains—Dorrada had plenty of them—but these were not like the familiar snow-capped peaks of home…these were stark, forbidding.

'The Jagros Mountains.' Zahir followed her gaze. 'They form the border between us and Uristan. They look deceptively close but there is a vast expanse of desert between us and them.'

Just as well. Annalina had no desire to visit them. She remembered, now that he said the name, that they were the mountains that had been the scene of terrible fighting during the war between Nabatean and Uristan.

'If you look over there…' With a jolt of surprise, Anna realised that Zahir had moved across the leather seat and was now right next to her. She registered the heat of his body, his scent, the sound of his breathing as he stretched one arm across her to point at an oval-shaped structure in the distance. 'You can see the new sports stadium. It's nearing completion now. Soon we will be able to host international sporting events. We intend to make a bid for the Olympics.'

Now the pride had crept into his voice. This

might be all about the people but there was no doubt what this country meant to Zahir.

'That's very impressive.' His nearness had caught the breath in her throat and she swallowed noisily. How was it that this man affected her so viscerally, so earthily? In a place deep down that she had never even known existed before?

She was grateful when the limousine finally pulled up outside the Assembly House and she was able to escape from its confines. Escape the pull of Zahir's power.

The meeting was as long as it was boring. Having been introduced to large numbers of dignitaries and advisors, Anna was then given the option of returning to the palace whilst the men—because it was all men—continued with the business of the day. But stubbornness and a vague hope that she might understand some of what they were discussing, that she would get a small insight into the running of Nabatean, made her say she would like to stay. In point of fact, even though the meeting was conducted in English, the items on the agenda were far too complicated for her to get a grip on, and she ended up staring out of the window or sneaking sidelong glances at Zahir as he controlled the proceedings with masterful authority. There was no sign of his brother at the meeting, or even any mention of him. It appeared that Zahir was the man in charge here. The power behind the throne.

They were standing at the top of a short flight of steps, preparing to leave the building, when Zahir suddenly stopped short, unexpectedly moving his arm around Anna's waist to pull her to his side. Looking outside, Anna could see a small crowd of people had gathered, leaning up against the ornate railings, peering up at the building expectantly.

Pulling out his phone, Zahir barked orders into it and from nowhere several security guards appeared. Dispatching a couple of them into the crowd, he waited impatiently, his grip around her waist tightening with every passing second. Anna could see a vein pulsing in his neck as his eyes darted over the crowd, missing nothing, a sudden stillness setting his features in stone. He reminded her of a dog on a leash, waiting to be set free to chase its quarry.

'What is it? What's the matter?'

'That's what I'd like to find out.'

The security guards returned and there was a brief conversation, during which she saw Zahir scowl, then look back at her with obvious contempt.

'It would seem that the crowd are here to see you.'

'Oh.' Anna stood a little straighter, smoothing the creases of her dress. 'That's nice.'

'Nice?' He repeated the word as if it was poison in his mouth. 'I fail to see what's nice about it.'

'Well, it's not surprising that people want to meet me. They are bound to be curious about your fiancée. I suggest we go out there, shake some hands and say hello.'

'We will do no such thing.'

'Why ever not?'

'Because there is a time and a place for such things. I have no intention of doing an impromptu meet-and-greet on the steps of the Assembly House.'

'These things don't always have to be formal, Zahir. It doesn't work like that.'

'In Nabatean things work the way I say they will work.'

Anna bit down hard on her lip. There really was no answer to that.

'And, quite apart from anything else, there is the security issue.'

'Well, they don't look dangerous to me.' Staring out at the swelling crowd, Anna stood her ground. 'And besides…' she glanced at the security guards around them '… I'm sure these guys are more than capable of dealing with any potential trouble.'

'There will be no trouble. We walk out of here and get straight into the limousine without speaking to anyone—without even looking at anyone. Do I make myself clear?'

'Crystal clear.' Anna shot him an icy glare. Not that she intended to follow his dictate. If she wanted to smile at the crowd, maybe offer a little wave, she jolly well would. Who did he think he was with his stupid rules?

But before she had the chance to do anything she found herself being bundled down the steps, pressed so closely to Zahir's side that she could barely breathe, let alone acknowledge the crowd. She could just about hear their cheers, hear them calling her name, before Zahir, with his hand on the back of her head, pushed her into the car, following behind her with the weight of his body and instructing the driver to move off before the car door was even shut.

'For heaven's sake.' Anna turned to look at him, eyes flashing. 'What was all that about?'

Adjusting the sleeves of his jacket, Zahir sat back, staring straight ahead.

'Anyone would think you were ashamed of me, bundling me into the car like a criminal.'

'Not ashamed of you, Annalina. It was simply a question of getting you into the car as fast as possible and with the minimum of harassment.'

'The only person harassing me was you. That was a few people—*your* people, I might add—who wanted to greet us. If you want real harassment, you should try having thirty or forty paparazzi swarming around you, baying for your blood.'

Zahir shot her a sharp glance. 'And this has happened to you?'

'Yes.' Anna shifted in her seat, suddenly uncomfortable with this subject, especially as Zahir's eyes were now trained on her face, waiting for an explanation. 'When my engagement to Prince Henrik ended.' She lowered her voice. 'And other times too. Though, that was the worst.'

'Well, you will never have to endure such indignity again. I will make sure of that.'

Anna turned to look out of the window, her hands clasped in her lap. He spoke with such authority, such confidence, she had to admit it was comforting. All her life she'd felt as if she was on her own, fighting her own battles, facing up to the trials and traumas, of which she'd suffered more than her fair share, without anyone there to help her, to be on her side. Now, it seemed, she had a protector.

Suddenly she knew she could put her trust

in Zahir, that she would put her life in his hands without a second thought, for that matter. Whether it was the paparazzi, a marauding army or a herd of stampeding elephants, come to that, he would deal with it. Such was his presence, the sheer overwhelming power of him. But the flip side was that he was also an arrogant, cold-blooded control freak. And one, Anna was shocked to realise, who was starting to dominate her every thought.

The rest of the journey back was conducted in silence, apart from the sound of Zahir's fingers jabbing at his mobile phone. Only when they were nearing the palace gates did he look up, letting out a curse under his breath. For there was a crowd here too, gathered around the palace gates, including some photographers who had climbed up onto the railings to get a better view.

'Dear God.' Zahir growled under his breath. 'Is this what I have to expect now, every time I leave the palace, every time I go anywhere with you?'

'I don't see your problem with it.' Anna twitched haughtily. 'You should be pleased that the people of Nabatean are interested in us. That they have gone to the trouble of coming to see us. Don't you want to be popular, for people to like you?'

'I don't care a damn whether people like me or not.'

'Well, maybe it's time you started to care.'

There—that had told him. Even so she averted her gaze, having no wish to witness the thunder she knew she would see there. Sitting up straighter, she arranged her hair over her shoulders. The palace gates had opened now and as the crowd parted to let their car through she turned to look out of the window and smiled brightly at everyone, giving a regal wave, the way she had been taught to do as a child. The crowd cheered in response, waving back and calling her name. Small children were held aloft to get a glimpse of her. Cameras flashed. Everybody loved it.

Well, not exactly everybody. A quick glance at her fiancé revealed a scowl that would make a tiger turn tail and run. But Anna refused to be cowed. She had done nothing wrong. Zahir Zahani was the one who needed to lighten up, respect his people by acknowledging their presence. Maybe even look as if he was a tiny bit proud of her. Though there was precious little chance of that.

Once inside, Zahir started to stride away, presumably intending to abandon her once again. But Anna had had enough of this. Taking several quick steps to catch up with him, she reached out, the touch of her hand on his arm stopping him in his tracks.

'I was just wondering…' She hesitated, pulling away her hand. 'Whether we would be having dinner together tonight.'

Zahir scowled, as if the possibility had hitherto never entered his mind. 'Dinner?'

'Yes.' She was tempted to point out that it was the meal at the end of the day that civilised people tended to share together. Self-preservation made her hold her tongue.

'That's not something I had planned.'

Picking up a length of hair, Anna curled it around her finger, suddenly hesitant. 'When you invite someone to your home, it's generally expected that you make some effort to entertain them. That is the role of a host. It's not much fun being left to rattle around here on my own.'

Deep brown eyes caught hers. 'I can see there are a couple of things I need to remind you of, Princess Annalina.' His sensuous mouth flattened into a grim line. 'Firstly, whilst it is true that you are a guest at the palace, I am most certainly not responsible for entertaining you. And, secondly, you should think yourself grateful that you have the freedom to *rattle around* on your own. The alternative would be to secure you in one room, have you watched over day and night. Something I did consider.'

'Don't be ridiculous.' Anna stared at him in horror.

Zahir gave an infuriating shrug. 'So perhaps you should see your freedom for what it is—a chance to prove yourself trustworthy—rather than complain about being neglected.'

Well, that was her put firmly in her place. Cheeks burning, she turned away, wishing she had never mentioned having wretched dinner with this wretched man.

'However, if it would please you, I can find time for us to dine together tonight. Shall we say in one hour's time?'

Anna swung round to face him again, the words *don't bother* tingling on her lips. But there was something about the narrowed gaze of those hooded eyes that made her stop.

It was surprise, she realised. Zahir was surprised that she wanted to any spend time with him. She was surprised too, come to that. It was like he had some sort of power over her, drawing her to the edge of the cliff when all her instincts were telling her to keep away. That blatant, raw masculinity made her keep coming back for more punishment. Anna had never thought of herself as a masochist. Now she was beginning to wonder.

Nervously licking her lips with the tip of her tongue, she saw his eyes flash in response, tightening the tendrils inside her. 'Very well.' Pushing back her shoulders, she tossed her hair over them. 'I will see you later.'

CHAPTER FIVE

ZAHIR STARED AT the young woman at the far end of the table—the European princess who was soon to be his bride. Something he was still desperately struggling to come to terms with. He had no idea who she was, not really. Earlier, when she'd talked about the press attention she'd received over the years, his blood had run cold in his veins. But fear about her morals had swiftly changed to the urge to protect her, his whole person affronted that she should ever have been subjected to such assaults. Because deep down some instinct told him that Princess Annalina was vulnerable and certainly not a woman who would give away her favours easily. Which was odd, when you thought about the way they had met.

She was certainly regal. From the fine bones of her face to the dainty set of her shoulders and the elegant, refined posture. Her hands, he noticed, were particularly delicate, long, slender fingers and pink nails devoid of nail varnish. They looked as if they had never done a day's work in their life. They probably hadn't.

He looked down at his own hands. A warrior's hands. No longer calloused from combat—he hadn't gripped a dagger or curled his finger around the trigger of a gun for over two years now—they were nevertheless stained with the blood of war and always would be. They had been around the throat of too many of his enemies ever to be washed clean—had been used to pull lifeless bodies out caves that had become subterranean battlegrounds, or recover corpses shrivelling in the scorching heat of the desert with the vultures circling overhead.

His hands had closed the eyelids of far too many young men.

And now… Could such hands ever expect to run over the fair skin of the woman before him? Would that be right? Permissible? They wanted to, that was for certain. They itched, burned even, with longing to feel the softness of her pale flesh beneath their fingertips, to be able to trace the contours of her slender body, to travel over the hollow of her waist, the swell of her breasts. They longed to explore every part of her body.

Feeling his eyes on her, Annalina looked up and smiled at him from her end of the table.

'This is delicious.' She indicated the half-eaten plate of food before her with the fork in her hand. 'Lovely and spicy. What's the meat, do you suppose?'

Zahir glanced down at his plate, already scraped clean, as if seeing it for the first time. Food was just fuel to him, something to be grateful for but to be consumed as fast as possible, before it was covered in flies or snatched away by a hungry hound. It was certainly not a subject he ever discussed, nor wanted to.

'Goat, I believe.' He levelled dark eyes at her.

'Oh.' That perfect pink mouth puckered in surprise then pursed shut, her fork left to rest on her plate.

He stifled a smile. Obviously goat was not something she was accustomed to eating. No doubt Annalina was more used to seeing them grazing prettily in wildflower meadows than having them stewed and presented before her in a bowl of couscous. She knew nothing of the ways of this country, he realised, and the smile was immediately replaced with the more familiar scowl.

Had he been wrong to insist that she marry him, to bring her to this foreign land and expect her to be able to fit in, play the role of his wife? It was a huge undertaking to ask of anyone, let alone someone as fragile-looking as her. And yet he already knew that there was more to

Annalina than her flawless beauty might suggest. She was strong-willed and she was brave. It had taken real guts to refuse to marry his brother, to stand on that bridge and do whatever she thought it took to get her out of that marriage. To kiss a total stranger. A kiss that still burned on his lips.

It had all backfired, of course. She had leapt straight from the frying pan into the fire, finding herself shackled to him instead. He was nothing like his brother, it was true. But, in terms of a husband, had Annalina made the right choice? Would she have been better sticking with the relative calm of Rashid, his particular demons regulated by carefully prescribed medication?

Or Zahir, whose demons still swirled inside him, drove him on, made him the man he was. Power, control and the overwhelming desire to do the best for his country was the only therapy he could tolerate.

He didn't know, but either way it was too late now. The choice had been made. They were both going to have to live with it.

'I hope I haven't spoiled your appetite?' The food, he noticed, had now been abandoned, Annalina's slender hand gripping the stem of her glass as she took a sip of wine, then another.

'No, it's not that.' She gave an unconvincing smile. 'It's actually quite filling.'

'Then, if you have finished, perhaps you would like to be served coffee somewhere more comfortable.'

'Um, yes, that sounds a good idea.' She touched a napkin to her lips. 'Where were you thinking of?'

'I will take mine in my quarters, but there are any number of seating areas in the palace that are suitable for relaxation. The courtyards are very pleasant too, though they will be chilly at this time of night.'

'I'm sure.' She fiddled with a tendril of hair that had escaped the swept-up style. 'Actually, I think I will join you.' There was determination in her voice, but vulnerability too, as if she might easily crack or splinter if challenged. 'I would like to see your quarters.'

Zahir stilled, something akin to panic creeping over him. He hadn't intended to invite her to his rooms. Far from it. By suggesting that they took their coffee elsewhere, he had been trying to escape from her. Which begged the question, why? Why would he, a man who would take on a band of armed insurgents with the bravery of a thousand warriors combined, be frightened by the thought of sharing a cup of coffee with this young woman? It was ridiculous.

Because he didn't know how to behave around her, that was why. This relationship had been thrust upon him so suddenly that he hadn't had time to figure out how to make it work, how to control it. And being around Annalina only seemed to make the task more difficult. Rather than clarifying the situation, she seemed to mess with his judgement. He found himself torn two ways—one side warning that he must be on his guard, and watch over this wayward princess like a hawk to make sure she didn't try to abscond, while the other side was instructing him to take her to his bed and make her his, officially.

The latter was a tempting prospect for sure. And the way she was looking at him now, eyes shining brightly as she held his gaze, her hands steepled under her chin, fingertips grazing her lips, it would take all his self-control not to give in to it. But control it he would, because control was something he prided himself on. More than that, something he ruled his life by, using it both to drive himself on and deny himself pleasure. Because pleasure was nothing but an indulgence, a form of weakness, a slippery slope that led down to the bowels of hell. That he had discovered to his cost with the most tragic of results: the murder of his parents.

On the eve of his country's independence he had been in a rowdy bar, watching, if not actually participating, as his brave comrades had celebrated their tremendous victory with flowing alcohol and loose women. He had been relaxed, enjoying himself, accepting the accolades, full of pride for what he had achieved. And all the time, a few hundred miles away, his parents were being murdered, a knife being drawn across their throats. A tragedy that he would never, *ever* begin to forgive himself for.

But that didn't stop the weight of lust in his groin grow heavier by the second, spreading its traitorous warmth through his body as he stared back at Annalina's open, inviting face. He had no idea why she was looking at him in that way. The workings of a woman's mind were a complete mystery to him, and not something he had ever thought he would care to concern himself with. But now he found he longed to know what was going on behind those eyes that were glazed perhaps a little too brightly—found that he would pay good money to find out what was going through that clever, complicated mind of hers.

'I doubt you will find anything remotely interesting about my quarters.'

'You will be in them. That's interesting enough for me.'

There she went again, throwing him a curve-ball, messing with his head. Was she flirting with him? Was that what this was? Zahir had experienced flirting before. His position of power, not to mention his dark good looks, meant he had had his fair share of female attention over the years. Most, but not all, of which he had totally ignored. He was a red-blooded male, after all. Occasionally he would allow himself to slake his thirst. But that was all it had ever been. No emotion, no attachment and certainly no second-guessing what the object of his attentions might be thinking. The way he found himself puzzling now.

'Very well. If you insist.' Summoning one of the hovering waiting staff with a wave of his hand, he gave his orders then, walking round to the back of Annalina's chair, he waited as she rose to her feet. 'If you would like to follow me.'

Setting off at a rapid pace, he found he had to moderate his step in order for Annalina to keep up. She trotted along beside him, her heels clicking on the marble floors, looking around her as if trying to memorise the route back in case she should need to escape. Zahir found himself regretting his decision to allow her into his rooms more and more with every forceful footstep. No woman, other than the palace staff, had ever been in his chambers. There had been no need for it. There was no need for it now. Why had he ever agreed to let this woman invade his personal space?

By the time they had negotiated the labyrinth of corridors and he was inserting the key into the lock of his door, Zahir's mood had blackened still further.

'You lock your door?' Waiting beside him, Annalina looked up in surprise.

'Of course. Security is of paramount importance.'

'Even in your own palace? There are guards everywhere. Do you not trust them to protect your property?'

'Trust no one and you will not be disappointed.' Zahir pushed hard on the heavy door with the palm of his hand.

'Oh, Zahir, that's such a depressing ideology!' Annalina attempted a throwaway laugh but it fell, uncaught, to the ground.

'Depressing it may be.' He stood back to let her enter. 'But I know it to be true.'

Taking in a deep breath, Anna stepped over the threshold. This was not going well. Maybe it had been a mistake to ask to accompany Zahir to his quarters. It had certainly done nothing to improve his mood. The resolve she had had at the start of the evening, to sit down and talk, try to get to know him a bit, discuss their future, had been severely tested during the course of the torturous meal. Every topic of conversation she had tried to initiate had either been met with cool disregard or monosyllabic answers.

All except one. When she had mentioned his parents, tried to tell him how sorry she was to hear of their tragic death, the look on Zahir's face had been terrifying to behold, startling her with its volcanic ferocity. It was clear that subject was most definitely off-limits.

But, where their future was concerned, she had to persevere. She needed to find out what was expected of her, what her role would be. And, more importantly, she needed to tell Zahir about herself, her shameful secret. Before it was too late. Which was why at the end of the meal she had fought against every instinct to turn tail and run to the safety of her bed and had persuaded him to bring her here. And why she found herself being welcomed into his spartan quarters with the all the enthusiasm that would have been given to a jester at a funeral.

For spartan it certainly was. In stark contrast to the rest of the palace, the room she was ushered into was small and dimly lit, with bare floorboards and a low ceiling. There was very little furniture, just a low wooden table and a makeshift seating area covered with tribal rugs.

'As I said.' Briefly following her gaze, Zahir moved to put the key in the lock on this side. He didn't turn it, Anna noticed with relief. 'There is nothing to see here.'

'Something doesn't have to be all glitz and glamour for it to be interesting, you know.' She purposefully took several steps into the room and, placing her hands on her hips, looked around her, displaying what she hoped was a suitably interested expression. 'How many rooms do you have here?'

'Three. This room, an office and a bedroom. Plus a bathroom, of course. I find that to be perfectly adequate.'

'Is this the bedroom?' Nervous energy saw her stride over to an open door in the corner of the room and peer in. In the near darkness she could just about make out the shape of a small bed, low to the ground, rugs scattered on the bare boards of the floor.

So this was where he slept. Anna pictured him, gloriously naked beneath the simple covers of this bed. He was so vital, so very much alive, that it was hard to imagine him doing anything as normal as sleeping. But she wouldn't allow herself to imagine him doing anything else. At least, not with anyone else.

'You obviously don't go in for luxuries here.'

'I do not. The basics are all I need. I find anything else is just an unwanted distraction.'

As was she, no doubt. Anna tamped down the depressing thought. 'So why build a palace like this, then? What's the point?'

'Medira Palace is for the people, a symbol of the power and wealth of Nabatean, something that they can look upon with pride. I may not choose to indulge in its luxuries, but it's not about me. The palace will be here for many generations after I have gone. And, besides, it's not just my home. My brother lives here too, as of course will you.'

'Yes.' Anna swallowed.

'You have no need to worry.' Zahir gave a harsh laugh. 'I don't expect you to share these chambers. You may have the pick of the rooms of the palace, as many and as grand as you wish.'

'And what about you? Will you be giving up these chambers and coming to live in splendour with me?'

'I will not.' Zahir's reply was as bleak as it was damning. What did that mean—that they would inhabit different parts of the palace? That they would live totally separate lives, be man and wife in name only? A knock on the door meant that Anna had to keep this deeply depressing thought to herself for the time being, as a servant bearing a tray of coffee saved Zahir from further questioning. Bending down, she settled herself as best she could on the low seating area, tucking her legs under her before reaching to accept her cup of coffee from the silent servant. It was impossible to get comfortable in her high-heeled shoes so, with her coffee cup balanced in one hand, she took them off with the other, pairing them neatly on the floor beside her. For some reason they suddenly looked ridiculously out of place, like twin sirens in the stark masculinity of this room.

Raising her eyes, Anna saw that Zahir was staring at them too, as if thinking the same thing. She was relieved when he roughly pulled off his own soft leather shoes and sat down beside her.

'So your brother.' She decided to opt for what she hoped was a slightly safer topic of conversation, but as she felt Zahir stiffen beside her she began to wonder. 'You say he lives here in the palace and yet I haven't seen any sign of him.'

'There is no reason for you to have seen him, as he occupies the east wing. Given the circumstances, I doubt that either of you are going to deliberately seek each other out.'

'Well, no.' Annalina pouted slightly. 'Having said that, I don't believe he wished to marry me any more than I did him.'

She waited, pride almost wishing that Zahir would contradict her, tell her that of course Rashid had wanted to marry her, 'what man wouldn't?'.

Instead there was only a telling silence as Zahir drank the contents of his coffee cup in one gulp then reached for the brass pot to refill it.

'There is some truth in that.' Avoiding her gaze, he eventually spoke.

Being right had never felt less rewarding. Drawing in a breath, Anna decided to ask the question that had been niggling her ever since she had first set eyes on Rashid Zahani. 'Can I ask…about Rashid… Is there some sort of medical problem?'

That spun Zahir's head in her direction, the dark eyes flashing dangerously beneath the thick, untidy eyebrows. So close now, Anna could see the amber flecks that radiated from the black pupils, glowing as if they were just about to burst into flames.

'So what are you saying? That anyone who doesn't want to marry you must have some sort of mental deficiency?' Scorn singed the edges of his words.

'No, I just…'

'Because if so you have a very high, not to say misguided, opinion of yourself.'

'That's not fair!' Colour rushed to flush Anna's cheeks, heating her core as indignation and embarrassment took hold. 'That's not what I meant and you know it.'

'Well, that's what it sounded like.' He looked away and she was left staring at his harsh profile, at the muscle that twitched ominously beneath the stubble of his cheek. There was silence as she battled to control the mixed emotions rioting inside her, as she waited for her skin to cool down.

'My brother has some personal issues to overcome.' Finally Zahir spoke again, leaning forward to replace his cup on the table. 'He suffers from anxiety due to a trauma he suffered and this can affect his mood. He just needs time, that's all. When the right person is found, he will marry and produce a family. Of that I am certain.'

'Of course.' Anna was not going to make the mistake of questioning that statement, even if secretly she had her doubts. There was something about Rashid that she found very unnerving. On the plane journey here she had looked up to see him staring at her in a very peculiar way, almost as if he was looking right through her. 'But does Rashid not get to choose his own wife? You make it sound as if he has no say in the matter.'

'Like me, you mean?' The eyes swung back, lingering this time, tracing a trail over her sensitised skin, across her cheekbones and down her nose, until they rested on her lips. Anna felt their burn as vividly as if she had been touched by a flame.

'And me too.' She just about managed to croak out the words of defiance, even though her heart had gone off like a grenade inside her.

'Indeed.' Something approaching empathy softened his voice. 'We are all victims of circumstance to a greater or lesser extent.'

Greater—definitely greater in her case. To marry this man, tie herself for ever to this wild, untamed, warrior, had meant taking the biggest leap of faith in her life. But Anna didn't regret it. In the same way as some inner sense had told her that she could never have married Rashid Zahani, it now filled her with nervous excitement at the thought of marrying his brother. Excitement, exhilaration and terror all rolled into one breathtaking surge of adrenaline. But there was worry too—worry that maybe once Zahir knew all the facts he might no longer want to marry her. She was beginning to realise just how devastating that would be. Because she wanted Zahir. In every sense of the word. Drawing in a shaky breath, she decided she was going to have to just plunge in.

'About our marriage, Zahir.' She watched the play of his muscles across his back as he leant forward to refill his coffee cup again. 'There are things we need to discuss.'

'I've told you. I will leave all the arrangements to you. I have neither the time nor the interest to get involved.'

'I'm not talking about the arrangements.'

'What, then?' He settled back against the cushions, his eyes holding hers with a piercing intensity that made her feel like a specimen butterfly being pinned to a board.

She shifted nervously to make sure she still could. 'We need to talk about what sort of marriage it will be.'

'The usual, I imagine.'

'And what exactly does that mean?' Irritation and helplessness spiked her voice. 'There is nothing usual about this marriage, Zahir. From the fact that I have been swapped from one brother to another, to your disclosure just now that we won't be sharing the same rooms. None of it fits the term *usual*.'

Zahir gave that infuriating shrug, as if none of it was of any consequence to him.

'Will you expect us to have full marital relations, for example?' She blurted out the question before she had time to phrase it properly, using language that sounded far more clinical than she felt. But maybe that was a good thing.

'Of course.' His straightforward answer, delivered in that raw, commanding voice and coupled with the burn of amber in those hooded eyes, had the peculiar effect of melting something inside of Anna, fusing her internal organs until she was aware of nothing but a deep pulse somewhere low down in her abdomen. It was a feeling so extraordinary, so remarkable, that she found she wanted to hold on to it, capture it, before it slipped away for ever.

Zahir intended that they should have sex. That in itself was hardly surprising, considering that they were going to be man and wife. Why had it sent her body into a clenching spasm?

'Nabatean is a young country. It is our duty to procreate, to provide a workforce for the future, to build upon the foundations we have established.' Ah, yes: *duty*. They were back to that again. 'But I don't intend to make constant demands on you.' He paused, thick lashes lowering to partly obscure his eyes. 'If that is what you're worrying about.'

Did she look worried? Anna had no idea what expression her face was pulling—she was too busy trying to control her body. And the thought of him making constant demands on her was only intensifying the peculiar feeling inside her. She needed to get a grip, and fast.

'In that case…there is something that you need to know. Before we get married, I mean.'

'Go on.'

Suddenly her whole body was painfully alive to him, every pore of her skin prickling with agonising awareness. The hairs on her arms, on the back of her neck, stood on end with craving, desire and the tortured anxiety of what she had to tell him.

'I'm not sure.' She reached for the security of a tendril of hair, twisting it round and round her finger. 'But it's quite possible that I am not able to…'

'Not able to what?'

'Not able to actually have sexual intercourse.'

CHAPTER SIX

ZAHIR'S DARK BROWS LOWERED, narrowing his hooded gaze until it was little more than twin slits of glinting stone. He twisted slightly so that his knee now touched hers, moving one arm behind them and placing it palm down on the cushions so that it anchored him in place. Anna could sense it, like a rod of muscled strength, inert yet still exuding power. Even seated he was so much taller than her, so much bigger, that she felt dwarfed by him, shaded, as if weakened by his strength.

'I don't understand.' He stared at her full in the face, with no trace of embarrassment or sensitivity for her predicament. She had presented him with a problem, that much was clear from the brooding intensity of his gaze, but it was a determination to get to the facts that had set his face in stone. 'What do you mean, you can't have sexual intercourse? Do you have some sort of physical abnormality?'

'No!' Anna pulled at the neckline of her dress, hoping it would dislodge the lump in her throat as well as cool herself down. The temperature in the small room seemed to have ramped up enormously. 'At least, it wouldn't appear so.'

'Have you been examined by a physician?'

'Yes, I have, actually.'

'And what were the findings?'

'They could find no physical reason for the… problem.'

'So what, then? What are you trying to tell me?'

'I'm trying to tell you that, when it actually comes to…you know… I can't actually… I fear I'm not able to accommodate a man.' Anna finished the sentence all in a rush, lowering her eyes against the shame that was sweeping over her that she should have to confess such a thing to the most virile, the most sexually charged, man she had ever met. A man who was now no doubt about to break off their short engagement.

There was a brief silence punctuated by Zahir's shallow breathing.

'Can I ask what has led you to this conclusion?'

Oh, God. Anna just wanted to make this hell go away. To make Zahir and the problem and the whole miserable issue of having sex at all just disappear. Why couldn't she just forget men, and getting married, and go and live in spinster isolation with nothing but a couple of undemanding cats for company? But beside her Zahir was waiting, the small amount of space between them shimmering with his impatient quest for information. There was nothing for it. She was going to have to tell him.

'Prince Henrik and I…' She paused, cringing inside. 'We never consummated our betrothal. You might as well know, that was why he broke off our engagement.'

'I wasn't aware that that was a prerequisite of a fiancée.' His eyes scoured her face. 'A wife, yes, but surely before marriage a woman is at liberty to withhold her favours?'

'That's just it, I didn't deliberately withhold them. It turned out that I was completely…unsatisfactory.'

'So let me get this straight.' *Oh, dear Lord*, still Zahir persisted with his questions. Couldn't he let it drop now? In a minute he would be asking her to draw him a diagram. 'You wanted to have sex with your fiancé but for some reason you weren't able?'

'Yes, well, sort of.' Since he had posed the question so baldly, Anna was forced to accept that she hadn't actually wanted to have sex with

Henrik at all. In fact, the thought of his pallid, sweaty hands fumbling around her most intimate areas still made her feel a bit sick. But the point was it had been expected of her. And she had failed.

'It was more Henrik's idea. He said it was important that we consummated our relationship before the wedding. "Try before you buy", I believe was his expression.'

Zahir's lip curled with distaste.

'And, as it turned out, it was just as well he did.'

This produced a low growl, like the rumble of a hungry lion, then a silence that Anna felt compelled to fill.

'I just thought you ought to know. Before we marry, I mean. In case it might prove to be a problem for us.'

'And do you think it will, Annalina?' Leaning forward, Zahir stretched out a hand to tuck a stray lock of hair behind her ear, his touch surprisingly gentle. Then, holding her chin between his finger and thumb, he tilted her face so that she had no alternative but to gaze into those bitter-chocolate eyes. 'Do you think it will be a problem for us?'

With her whole body going into paralysis, including the beat of her heart and pump of her lungs, it was quite possible that staying alive might prove to be a problem. She stared at the sweep of his jawline—the one facial feature that probably defined him more than any other. As if hewn from granite, it was as uncompromising and as harshly beautiful as him. There was an indentation in the squared-off chin, she noted—not a dimple. A man like Zahir Zahani would never be in possession of a dimple. A strong dusting of stubble shaded its planes.

On the bridge in Paris, when she had so recklessly decided to kiss him, she had been dimly aware that his skin had felt smooth, freshly shaved. But how would it would feel tonight, now, with that tempting shadow of dark beard? Suddenly she longed to find out, to feel it rasp against her cheek like the lick of a cat's tongue. He was so very close…so very difficult to resist.

'I don't know.' Finally finding her voice, Anna blinked against the erotic temptation. That was the truth: she didn't. Right now she didn't know anything at all. Except that she wanted Zahir to kiss her more than anything, more than she cared about her next breath. She found herself unconsciously squirming on the makeshift sofa, the rough weave of the tribal rugs scratching the exposed bare skin of her thigh as her dress rode up.

What was she doing? This had not been her plan at all. When she had summoned up her courage, faced Zahir with her guilty, frankly embarrassing, secret, it had been with the intention of letting him know what he was taking on here. That his fiancée was frigid. Anna still felt the pain of the word, hurled at her by Henrik as he had levered his body off her, before pulling on his clothes and storming off into the night. *Frigid.*

His accusation had torn into her, flaying her skin, leaving her staring up at the ceiling in horrified confusion. Not to be able to perform the most basic, natural function of a woman was devastating. She was inadequate, useless. Not a proper woman at all, in fact. The doctor's diagnosis hadn't helped. Being told there was nothing physically wrong with her, that there was no quick fix—no medical fix at all, in fact—had only added to her lack of self-worth. Neither had time softened the blow, her deficiency seeping into her pride and her confidence, leaving her feeling empty, like a hollow shell.

So what on earth was she doing now? Why was she writhing about like some sort of temptress, trying to get Zahir's attention, setting herself up for what was bound to be a painful and embarrassing fall? Because she wanted him, that was why. She wanted his lips against hers, touching, tasting, crushing her mouth, sucking the breath out of her until she was gasping for air. She wanted him to make her feel. The way no one ever had before. The way she now knew with a dizzying certainty that he could.

Zahir stared into Annalina's flushed face that he still held tilted up towards him. At the eyes that were heavy with a drugging sense of what appeared to be arousal. And once again he found himself wondering what the hell was going on in her head. If she had been flirting with him earlier on, this felt more like full-on seduction. And this after she had just told him she was incapable of sexual intercourse. It didn't make any sense. But neither did the drag of lust that was weighing down his bones, making it impossible to move away from her, or the prickle of heat that had swept through his body, like he'd been plugged into the national grid. He could feel it now, right down to his finger tips that were tingling against the soft skin of her chin.

And there was something else bothering him too. It had been building ever since Annalina had started to talk about this ex-fiancé of hers, Prince Henrik, or whatever his wretched name was. Just the thought of him touching Annalina, *his* Annalina, had sent his blood pressure rocketing. By the time she'd got to the bit about them not being able to consummate their relationship, he had been ready to tear the man limb from limb, happy to chuck the remains of his mutilated body to the vultures without a backward glance. And this aggression for a man he had never met—nor ever would, if he wanted to avoid a life sentence for homicide. He could still feel the hatred seething inside him now: that such a man had dared to try and violate this beautiful creature, then discard her like a piece of trash. It had taken all of his self-control not to let Annalina see his revulsion.

Now Zahir spread his hand possessively under her jaw, his eyes still holding hers, neither of them able to break contact.

'There's one sure way to find out.' He heard his words through the roar of blood in his ears, the throb of it pulsing in his veins. Not that he was in any doubt. He knew he could take this beautiful princess and erase the memory of that spineless creep of a creature, take her to his bed and show her what a real man could do. Just the thought of it made his hands tremble and he pressed the pads of his thumbs against her skin to steady them, rhythmically stroking up and down. He watched her eyelashes flutter against his touch and the roar inside him grew louder.

He might not be able to read Anna's mind, but he could read her body, and that was all the encouragement he needed. The angle of her head, the slight arching of her back that pushed her breasts towards him, the soft rasp of her breath, all told him that she was his for the taking. That she wanted him every bit as much as he wanted her. Well, so be it. But this time the kiss would be on *his* terms.

He lowered his head until their mouths were only a fraction apart. *Now*, a voice inside his head commanded. And Zahir obeyed. Planting his lips firmly on Annalina's upturned pout, he felt its warm softness pucker beneath him and the resulting kick of lust in his gut momentarily halted him right there. He inhaled deeply through his nose. This was not going to be a gentle, persuasive kiss. This was going to be hot and heavy and hardcore. This was about possession, domination, a man's need for a woman. His need for her right now.

He angled his head to be able to plunder more deeply, the soft groan as her lips parted to allow him access only fuelling the fire that was raging through him. His tongue delved into the sensual cavern of her mouth, seeking her own with a brutal feverishness that saw it twist around its target, touching, tasting, taking total control, until Anna reciprocated, the lick of her tongue against his taking him to new fervid heights. Releasing her chin, Zahir moved his fingers to the back of her head, pushing them forcefully up through her hair, feeling the combs and grips that held the tresses in their swept-up style dislodge satisfyingly beneath his touch until the thick locks of blonde hair fell free, tumbling down through his fingers and over her shoulders.

Grabbing a handful of this glorious, silken wonder, Zahir used it to anchor her in place, to hold her exactly where he wanted her, so that he could increase the pressure on her mouth still further, increase the intensity of the kiss, heighten the pleasure that was riotously coursing through him. And, when Anna snaked her hands behind his neck, pressing herself against him, her breasts so soft, so feminine against the muscled wall of his chest, it was all he could do to stop himself from taking her right there and then. No questions asked, no thoughts, no deliberation, no cross-examination. Nothing but a blind desire to possess her in the most carnal way possible. To make her his.

Which would be totally wrong. Releasing her lips, Zahir pulled back, the breath heaving in his chest, the tightening in his groin almost unbearably painful. A kiss was one thing, but to take her virginity—for surely that was what they were talking about here?—was quite another. This wasn't the time or the place. And to do it merely to prove himself more of a man than Henrik would be morally reprehensible. Somehow, from somewhere, he was going to have to find some control.

The look of dazed desire in Annalina's eyes was almost enough to make him claim her again, blow his new-found resolve to smithereens. But within a split second her expression had changed and now he saw a wariness, a fear almost, and that was enough to bring him forcibly to his senses. Realising that he was still clutching a handful of her hair, he let it drop and pushed himself away until he found himself on his feet, staring down at her from a position of towering authority that he felt far more comfortable with.

'I apologise.' His voice sounded raw, unfamiliar, as alien to him as the wild sensations that were coursing through the rest of his body. Sensations that he realised would be all too evident if Annalina raised her eyes to his groin. He shifted his position, adjusting the fit of his trousers.

But Annalina wasn't looking at him. She was busy with her hair, combing her fingers through the blonde tresses, arranging it so that it fell over her shoulders. Then she leant forward to retrieve the clips that had fallen to the floor.

'What is there to be sorry for?' Now her eyes met his, cold, controlled, defiant. 'We are engaged, after all.' She held the largest clip in her hand, a hinged, tortoiseshell affair which now squeaked as she opened and closed its teeth, as if it was ready to take a bite out of him. 'You are perfectly at liberty to kiss me. To do whatever you like with me, in fact. At least, that's been the impression you have given me so far.'

There was rebellion in her voice now, matched by the arched posture, the arrogant, feline grace. But her lips, Zahir noticed, were still swollen from the force of their kiss, the delicate skin of her jaw flushed pink where his stubbled chin had scraped against her. And for some reason this gave him a twisted sense of achievement—as if he had marked his territory, claimed her. Especially as, now, everything about Annalina was trying to deny it.

'Perhaps you would do well to remember that this is all your doing, Annalina. You have brought about this situation and you only have yourself to blame. I am merely trying to find a workable solution.'

A solution that should not involve ripping the clothes off her the moment they were alone.

'I know, I know.' Rising to her feet, Annalina planted herself squarely in front of him, sticking out her bottom lip like a sulky teenager. Barefoot, she seemed ridiculously tiny, delicate, her temper making her brittle, as if she would snap in two were he to reach forward and grasp her with his warrior's hands.

'And, whilst we're on the subject of workable solutions, perhaps you would like to tell me how long I am expected to stay in Nabatean. I have duties in my own country, you know, matters that require my attention.'

'I'm sure.' Zahir gritted his jaw against the desire to close the small gap between them and punish her impertinence with another bruising kiss. 'In that case, no doubt you will be relieved to know that you'll be returning to Dorrada the day after tomorrow.'

'Oh, right.' Annalina shifted her weight lightly from one foot to the other, placing her hand provocatively on her hip. 'Well, that's good.'

'I have a number of meetings scheduled for tomorrow but have cleared my diary for the following couple of days.'

He watched, not without some satisfaction, as her frown of incomprehension turned to a scowl of realisation. Her toes, he noticed, were curling against the bare boards.

'You mean…?'

'Yes, Annalina. I will be accompanying you. I very much look forward to visiting your country.'

CHAPTER SEVEN

OPENING THE SHUTTERS, Anna shielded her eyes against the glare of the sun. Not the sun glinting off the towering glass edifices of Medira this time, or shimmering above the distant desert, but bouncing off the freshly fallen snow that blanketed the ground, weighing down the fir trees and covering the roofs of the town of Valduz that nestled in the valley in the distance.

She was back at Valduz Castle, the only home she had ever known. Perched on a craggy outcrop at the foothills of the Pyrenees mountain range, the castle was like something out of a fairy tale, or a Dracula movie, depending on your point of view. Built in the fourteenth century, it was all stone walls, turrets and battlements, fully prepared for any marauding invaders. It was not, however, prepared for the twenty-first century. Cold, damp and in desperate need of repair, its occupants—including Anna, her father and the bare minimum of staff—only inhabited a very small portion of it, living in a kind of squalid grandeur: priceless antique furniture had been pushed aside to make room for buckets to catch the drips, steel joists propping up ceilings decorated with stunning fifteenth-century frescoes.

But all this was about to change. Turning around, Anna surveyed her childhood bedroom in all its forlorn glory. Once she married Zahir, money would no longer be a problem for this impoverished nation. Valduz Castle would be restored, and limitless funds would be pumped into the Dorradian economy to improve its infrastructure, houses, hospitals and schools. Dorrada's problems would soon be over. *And hers would be just beginning.*

But she could feel no sense of achievement for her part in turning around Dorrada's fortunes. Instead there was just a hollow dread where maybe pride should have sat—a deep sense of unease that she had sold her soul to the devil. Or at least as close to a devil as she had ever come across. And that very devil was right here, under the leaking roofs of this ancient castle.

They had arrived in Dorrada the previous evening, her father greeting Zahir like an honoured guest, clearly having no concerns that his daughter was marrying the wrong brother.

The two of them had retired immediately to her father's study and that had been the last Anna had seen of them. Presumably the financial talks had been the top priority and had gone on long into the night. Anna was obviously of significantly less importance to either of them. Zahir, professional but detached, appeared to be treating this like just another business trip, all traces of the man who had been on the brink of ravishing her banished behind that formidable, impenetrable facade.

Anna closed her eyes against the memory of that kiss—hot, wild, and so forceful it had felt as if he was branding her with his lips, claiming her in the most carnal way. It still did. The memory refused to leave her, still curling her toes, clenching her stomach and heating her very core.

And Zahir had felt it too, no matter how much his subsequent demeanour might be trying to deny it. His arousal had been all too evident—electrifying, empowering. Trapped in his embrace, she had felt alive, confident, sexy. And ready. More than ready, in fact. Desperate for Zahir to take things further, to throw her to the floor and make love to her there and then, any way he wanted. To possess her, make her feel whole, complete, a real woman.

But what had happened? Nothing, that was

what. Having taken her to the point of no return, he had stopped, leaving her a quivering, gasping, flushed-faced mess, unable to do anything other than stare up at him as he bit out between gritted teeth that he was sorry. *Sorry?* Anna didn't want sorry. It had taken every ounce of effort to come back from that, to hide the crushing disappointment and act as if she didn't give a damn.

But today was a new day. She was on her own home turf, the sun was shining and the stunning scenery outside was calling her. Pulling on jeans and a thick roll-neck sweater, she released the curtain of hair trapped down her back and quickly fashioned two loose plaits. Grabbing a woolly hat, she was good to go.

The virgin snow crunched beneath her boots as she trudged around the wall of the castle, the white puff of her breath going before her. She didn't know exactly where she was headed, except that she wanted to enjoy this moment alone, commit it to memory. She loved mornings like this, bright and still, unchanged down the centuries. But how many more would she experience? No doubt once she was married she would be expected to spend all her time in Nabatean, to swap the sparkling cold of the mountains for the sweltering heat of the desert, the stark loneliness of her life here for the scary unknown that was her future with Zahir.

It was time to leave the child behind—Anna knew that. Time to grow up and do something meaningful with her life. And being born a princess meant making an advantageous marriage. She should have accepted the idea by now. After all, she'd had twenty-five years to get used to it. But even so, now it was actually happening, the thought of leaving everything she knew and marching off into the desert sun with this dark and mysterious stranger was completely terrifying.

The lingering child in her made her bend down and scoop up a large handful of snow, compacting it into a hard ball and then smoothing it between her icy hands. Her eyes scanned the scene for a target. A robin eyed her nervously before swooping off to the branches of a nearby tree. An urn at the top of the crenulated wall that wound its way down the stone steps had no such escape, though, and, taking aim, Anna held the icy missile aloft and prepared to fire.

'You'll never get any power behind it like that.' A strong, startlingly warm hand gripped her wrist, bringing her arm down by her side. 'Throwing is all about the velocity. You need to stand with your feet apart and then turn at the waist, like this.' The hands now spanned her midriff, twisting her body in readiness for the perfect aim. Anna tensed, staring at the snowball in her hand, frankly surprised to see it still there. The heat coursing through her body felt powerful enough to melt an iceberg. 'Now bring back your arm, like this…' he bent her elbow, holding her arm behind her '…and you are ready to go. Don't forget to follow through.'

The snowball arced above them before disappearing with a soft thud into a deep snowdrift.

'Hmm…' Turning to face her, Zahir quirked a thick brow. 'I can see more practice is needed.'

Anna stared back at him, drinking in the sight. He looked very foreign, exotic, in the bright, snowy whiteness of these surroundings. Wearing a long charcoal cashmere coat, the collar turned up, his skin appeared darker somehow, his close-cropped hair blacker, his broad body too warm—too hot, even—for these sub-zero temperatures. It was almost as if he could defy nature by appearing so unaffected by the cold. That you could remove the man from the desert, but not the desert from the man. Anna adjusted her hat, regretting her choice of headgear as she felt the silly bobble on top do a wobble. 'It's too late for me, I fear. After all, I won't be here for much longer.'

'Will you miss your country?' The question came out of nowhere with its usual directness. But his eyes showed his seriousness as he waited for her answer.

'Yes, of course.' Anna bit down on her lip, determined that the bobble on her hat was the only thing that was going to wobble. She would be strong now. Show Zahir that she was a capable, independent woman. That she would be an asset to him, not a burden. 'But I am looking forward to the challenges of a new life, with you. I am one hundred percent committed to making this union work, for the sake of both of our countries.'

'That's good to hear.' Still his gaze raked across her like a heat-seeking missile. 'And what about on a more personal level, Annalina? You and me. Are you one hundred percent committed to making that union work too?'

'Yes, of course.' Anna fought against the heat of his stare. What was he trying to do to her? She was struggling to put on a convincing performance here. She didn't need him messing with the script. 'I will try to be a good wife to you, to fulfil my duty to the best of my abilities.'

'*Duty*, Annalina. Is that what this is all about?'

'Well, yes. As it is with you.' Dark eyebrows raised and then fell again, taking Anna's stomach with them. 'But that doesn't mean we can't be happy.'

'Then you might want to tell your face.' Raising a hand, he cupped her jaw, his hand so large that it covered her chin and lower cheeks, seductively grazing her bottom lip. Anna trembled, his touch halting her cold breath painfully in her throat. 'What is it that you fear, Annalina? Is it the thought of tying yourself to a man such as myself? A man ignorant of the manners of Western culture, more at home in a desert sandstorm, or riding bareback on an Arab stallion, than making polite conversation in a grand salon or waltzing you around a palace ballroom?'

'No…it's not that.'

'I am not the cultured European prince you were hoping for?' Suddenly bitterness crept into his voice.

'No, it's not that, Zahir. Really.'

'What, then? I need to know.' The searing intensity in his eyes left her in no doubt about that. 'Do you fear that I am such a difficult man to please?' His voice dropped.

Yes. 'Impossible' might be a better word. Anna stared back at him, tracing the map of his face with her eyes: the grooves between eyebrows that were so used to being pulled into a scowl, the lines scored across a forehead that frowned all too easily. Had she ever even seen him smile? She wasn't sure. How did she have any hope of pleasing such a man?

'I fear I may need time to learn the ways to make you happy.' She chose her words carefully, trying to avoid snagging herself on the barbed wire all around her. Trying to conceal the inbuilt dread that she might not be able to satisfy him. Her abortive night of shame with Henrik still haunted her, plagued her with worry and self-doubt. And the way Zahir had dismissed it had done nothing to allay her fears either, merely demonstrated that he no idea of the scale of the problem. That he didn't understand.

'All being well, time is something we have plenty of, my princess.' The very masculine gleam in his eye only made Anna feel a hundred times worse. 'A lifetime together, in fact.'

'Yes, indeed. A lifetime…' Her voice tailed off.

'And learning to please one another need not be such an arduous task.' His thumb stroked over her lower lip.

'No, of course not.' Anna's heart took up a thumping beat. His gentle touch, the depth of his dark stare, spelled out exactly the sort of pleasure he was talking about: intimate, sexual pleasure. It shone in his eyes and it clenched deep down in Anna's belly.

She had spent so long worrying about how to satisfy Zahir that it hadn't even occurred to her that sex was a reciprocal thing. That he might be thinking of ways to pleasure her. Now hot bolts of desire ricocheted through her at the thought of it. Of Zahir's large rough-skinned hands travelling over her naked body, moving between her thighs, pushing them apart, spanning the mound of her sex before exploring within. A shiver of longing rippled through her and she had to squeeze her muscles tight to halt its progress.

'I must go.' Releasing her chin, Zahir let his thumb rest against her lip for a second, gently dragging it down. Then he took a step away. 'Your father has meetings arranged for me all morning. However, I have set aside this afternoon for us to spend some time together.'

'You have?' Anna couldn't keep the surprise from her voice, nor cover up the leap of excitement that coloured her cheeks.

'After your little lecture about the role of a host, I assume you will be willing to show me around Dorrada?'

'Yes, of course.'

'Time is limited—I leave for Nabatean first

thing tomorrow—but I should like to take in some of the sights before I go.'

'You're going back to Nabatean tomorrow?' This was news to her.

'Correct.'

'Alone?'

'I take it that won't be a problem?'

'Not for me, I can assure you.' Anna fiddled with one of her plaits. 'So does this mean you finally trust me or am I to be surrounded by your minders?'

'No minders.' Zahir narrowed his eyes as he contemplated her question. 'But trust is not something I find easy to give. Once you have suffered the sort of betrayal I have, it is hard to ever completely trust anyone again.'

'I'm sure.' Anna lowered her eyes. At first she had thought he was talking about her, what she had done on the bridge in Paris. But the pain in his eyes ran deeper than that, far deeper. She wanted to ask more but Zahir was already pulling down the shutters, aware that he had said too much.

'However, I'm prepared to give you the freedom to prove yourself.' He levelled dark eyes at her. 'Just make sure you don't let me down.'

'I suppose we should be getting back to the castle.' Night was starting to close in, the first stars appearing in the sky, and reluctantly Anna felt in her pocket for the car keys. Their whistle-stop tour of Dorrada was nearly over, something that disappointed Anna more than she would ever have imagined.

Zahir hadn't bothered to hide his surprise when she had pulled up in front of the castle in the battered old four-by-four vehicle and gestured to him to get in beside her. Warily easing himself into the passenger seat, he had shot her one of his now familiar hooded stares, leaving her in no doubt that this was a situation he did *not* feel comfortable with—whether that was being driven by a woman, or her in particular, she didn't know. And didn't care. She was a good driver, she knew the roads around here like the back of her hand, and the challenging conditions of this wintry climate posed no problems for her. And even if he'd looked as though he was coming perilously close to grabbing the wheel off her a couple of times—especially on some of the spectacular hairpin bends that snaked up through the mountains—he had just about managed to restrain himself, travelling every inch of the road with his eyes instead.

Deciding where to take her guest had been difficult. Dorrada was only a small country but the scenery was spectacular and there were so many places Anna would have liked to show him. But time was short so she had limited herself to a trip up into the mountains, with several stops to admire the views, including the place where an ancient cable car still vertiginously cranked tourists down to the valley below. Then she had given him a rapid tour of the town of Valduz, unable to stop because she'd known they would attract too much attention. People turned to stare at them as they passed anyway, rapidly pulling out their phones to take a photo, or just waving excitedly as their princess and her exotic fiancé drove by.

The last stop on Anna's tour had brought them to this mountain lakeside, one of her favourite places. Originally she hadn't intended to bring Zahir here but somehow it had happened and now she was glad of that. Because as they had crunched their way along the shoreline, stopped to take in the stunning sunset rippling across the crystal-clear water, she knew that Zahir was feeling the beauty of the place every bit as much as her. Not that he said so. Zahir was a man of few words, using communication as a mere necessity to have his wishes understood or his orders obeyed. But there had been a stillness as he'd gazed across the water to the snow-capped mountains beyond, an alertness in the way he'd held his body, that had told Anna how much he was feeling the magic of this place. They hadn't needed any words.

'There's no rush, is there?' Zahir turned to look at her, his face all sharp-angled lines and shadows in the dim light.

'Well, no, but it's getting dark. There's not much point in me taking you sightseeing if you can't see the sights.'

'I like the dark.' Zahir laid the statement baldly before her, as if it was all that was needed to be said. Anna didn't doubt it. She already thought of him a man of the night, a shadowed, stealthy predator that would stalk his prey—would curl his hands around the throat of an enemy before they even knew of his existence. 'Is that some sort of cabin over there between those trees?'

Anna followed his finger, which was pointing to the other side of the lake. 'Yes, it's an old hunter's cabin.'

'Shall we take a look?'

Anna hesitated. She didn't need to take a look, she was all too familiar with the modest cabin. She should be. She'd been escaping here for years, to her own little bolthole, whenever the bleak reality of her life in the castle got too much for her.

It was to here that she had fled all those years ago, on being told that her mother had died. That she would never see her again. Here, too, much more recently, she'd sat staring at the rustic walls, trying to come to terms with the fact that a marriage had been arranged for her. That she was to be shipped off to a place called Nabatean to marry the newly crowned king. And look how that had turned out.

The cabin was her secret place. Taking Zahir there would feel strange. But somehow exciting too.

'Sure, if you like.' Affecting a casual tone, she started walking. 'D'you want to follow me?'

They set off, Anna leading the way around the lake and into the fringes of the forest of pine trees. It was too dark to see much but she knew the way by heart. Zahir was right behind her every step, so close that they moved as almost one being, their feet crunching on snow that had crystallised to ice. She could sense the heat from his body, feel the power of it all around her. It made her feel both safe and jumpy at the same time, butterflies leaping about in her tummy.

Finally they came to a small clearing and there was the log cabin before them, looking like a life-size gingerbread house. The door was wedged shut by a drift of snow but with a few swift kicks Zahir had cleared it and soon they were both standing inside.

'There should be some matches here somewhere.' Running her hands over the table next to her, Anna opened the drawer, relieved to feel the box beneath her fingertips. 'I'll just light the paraffin lamp.'

'Here, let me.' Taking the matches from her Zahir reached up and, removing the glass funnel from the lamp, touched a flame to the wick. 'Hmm…' With a grunt of approval, he looked around him in the flickering light. 'Basic but perfectly functional. You say it was a hunter's cabin?'

'Yes, hence the trophies.' Anna pointed to the mounted deer heads that gazed down on them with glassy-eyed stares. 'But it hasn't been used for years. Valduz Castle used to host hunting parties in the past, but, thankfully for the local wildlife, those days have gone.'

'But you come here?'

'Well, yes, now and again.' Was it that obvious? His directness immediately put her on the defensive. 'I used to like it here as a kid. Other children had play houses and I had my own log cabin!' She attempted a light-hearted laugh but as the light played over Zahir's harsh features they showed no softening. He merely waited for her to elaborate. 'And now I sometimes come here when I want to think, you know? Get away from it all.'

'I understand.' The deep rumble of his voice, coupled with the hint of compassion in his dark eyes threatened to unravel something deep inside her.

'Shall we light a fire?' Hideously chirpy—she'd be asking him if he wanted to play mummies and daddies in a minute—Anna moved over to the open hearth. 'There should be plenty of logs.'

Immediately Zahir took charge, deftly getting the fire going with the efficiency of a man well used to such a task. Anna watched as he sat forward on his haunches, blowing onto the scraps of bark until the smoke turned to flames and the flames took hold. There was something primal about his movements. Hypnotic. Mission accomplished, he sat back on his heels.

'I think there's some brandy here somewhere if you'd like some?' Needing to break the spell, Anna moved over to a cupboard and pulled out a dusty bottle and a couple of tumblers.

'I never drink alcohol.'

'Oh.' Now she thought about it, she realised she had never seen him drink. 'Is that because of your religion or for some other reason?' She poured a modest amount into one glass.

'I don't believe in deliberately altering the state of my mind with toxic substances.'

Right. Anna glanced at the drink in her hand, sheer contrariness making her add another good measure before turning back to look around her. There was only one chair in the cabin, a rickety old wooden rocker, but the bare floor was scattered with animal skins and she moved to seat herself beside Zahir in front of the fire.

Zahir cast her a sideways glance, as if unsure how to deal with this situation, before finally settling his large frame beside her, sitting cross-legged and staring into the flames. For a moment there was silence, just the crackling of the logs. Anna took a gulp of brandy, screwing up her eyes against its burn.

'So.' She'd been tempted to remain quiet, to see how long it would be before Zahir instigated some sort of conversation, but she suspected that would be the wrong side of never. 'What do you think of Dorrada?'

'Its economy has been very badly handled. I fail to see how a country with such potential, such a noble history, can have got itself in such a mess.'

Anna pouted. If she'd been expecting a comment on the beauty of the scenery or the quality of the air, she should have known better. 'Well, we don't all have the benefit of gallons of crude oil gushing out of the ground. I'm sure it's easy to be a wealthy country when you have that as a natural resource.'

Spinning round, his jaw held rigid, Zahir's looked ready to take a bite out of her. 'If you think there has been anything remotely *easy* about reforming a nation like Nabatean then I would urge you to hastily reconsider. Nabatean has not been built on oil but on the spilt blood of its young men. Not on the value of its exports of but on the courage and strength of its people. You would do well to remember that.'

'I'm sorry.' Suitably chastened, Anna took another sip of brandy. Perhaps that had been a stupid thing to say. He had turned back towards the fire now, his whole body radiating his disapproval. 'I didn't mean any disrespect. I still know so little of the ways of your country.'

'You will have ample opportunity to learn our ways, our language and our ethos once you are living there. And may I remind you that Nabatean will shortly be *your* country too?'

'Yes, I know that.' Anna swallowed. 'And I will do my best to embrace the culture and learn all I can. But it would help me if you told me more about it now.'

Zahir shrugged broad shoulders.

'You say the war that brought about the independence of Nabatean cost many lives?'

'Indeed.' He shifted his weight beside her.

'And you yourself were in the army, fighting alongside your fellow countrymen?'

'Yes. As the second son, I always knew that the army would be my calling. It was an honour to serve my country.'

'But you must have seen some terrible atrocities.'

'War is one long atrocity. But sometimes it is the only answer.'

'And your parents…' Anna knew she was straying into dangerous territory here. 'I understand that they…died?'

'They were murdered, Annalina, as I am sure you well know. Their throats cut as they slept.' He stared into the flames as if transfixed. 'Less than twenty-four hours after Uristan had capitulated and the end of the war declared, they were dead. I was celebrating our victory with the people of Nabatean when a rebel insurgent took advantage of the lapse in security and crept into my parents' bedchamber to slaughter them as a final act of barbarity.'

'Oh, Zahir.' Anna's hands fluttered to her throat. 'How terrible. I'm so sorry.'

'It is I who should be sorry. It was my job to

protect them and I failed. I will carry that responsibility with me to my grave.'

'But you can't torture yourself with that for ever, Zahir. You can't carry all that burden on your shoulders.'

'Oh, but I can. And I will.' His jaw tightened. 'It was supposed to have been a safe house. I had only moved them out of exile a week before, along with my brother. I was convinced no one knew of their whereabouts. But I was betrayed by a guard I thought I could trust.'

'And your brother, Rashid? He obviously escaped the assassin?'

'He awoke to hear my mother screaming his name. Even with a knife at her throat, seconds from death and with her husband already slaughtered beside her, my mother managed to find enough strength to warn her son. To save him. But, had I been there, I could have saved them all. I *would* have saved them all.'

Anna didn't doubt it for one moment. There wasn't an armed assassin in the world that would stand a chance against someone like Zahir.

'Your mother sounds like an amazing woman.'

'She was.'

'And I'm sure she and your father would be very proud of what you have achieved. You and Rashid.'

'Rashid, as I am sure you are aware, has not yet fully recovered from his ordeal.' His held his profile steady, stark and uncompromising.

Anna hesitated, choosing her words with care. She had no desire to get her head bitten off again. 'And that's the reason you're governing the kingdom, rather than him?'

'My brother is happy to let me run the country as I see fit. His role is more that of a figurehead. He is temporarily unsuited to the rigours of leadership.'

So it was just as she thought. Zahir Zahani was the power and brains behind the success of Nabatean. She sat up a little straighter. 'I hope that you will allow me to assist you?' Determined that he should see some worth in her, she almost implored him. 'I'm a hard worker and a quick learner. I'm sure I have skills that you can utilise.'

'I'm sure you have.' Zahir turned towards her, his eyelids heavy, thick, dark lashes lowered. 'And I look forward to utilising them.'

The rasp of his words sent a tremor of anticipation through her. With the flames licking the shadows of his face, shining blue-black on his hair and gleaming in his eyes, she felt her heart pound, her body melt with the power of his raw sexual energy. There had been no mistaking the meaning behind his words. It pulsed from him, throbbed in the air between them, weakening her limbs with its promise.

Impulse made her reach for his cheek and gently run the back of her hand against it, feel the scratch of his stubble, the burn of the heat from the fire. Immediately he grasped her wrist, twisting her hand so that her fingers brushed his mouth and then, taking her index finger between his lips, holding it between his teeth, clenching down so that it was trapped, warm and damp from his breath, his bite hard but controlled. It was an action so unexpected, so intimate, and so deeply sexy that for a moment Anna could do nothing but stare at him, her whole body going into heart-stopping free fall.

She wanted more. She knew that with a certainty that thundered in her head, roared the blood in her ears and pulsed down low in her abdomen. She wanted him the way she had never wanted any other man in her life. She had no idea what would happen when it came to it, to the point where she had failed so pitifully before, but she knew she wanted to try. Right now.

CHAPTER EIGHT

THEIR GAZES CLASHED and Anna watched, spellbound, as the firelight danced across the surface of Zahir's black eyes. Slowly, seductively, his tongue licked the tip of her finger, sending a wave of pure lust crashing over her. She waited, desperate for him to suck it into his mouth, and when he released his teeth and did just that she closed her eyes and moaned with pleasure, revelling in the rasp of his tongue, the powerful suck of his mouth, the graze of his teeth against her knuckles.

She craved more, the thought of the suck of that mouth against other parts of her body…against her nipples, her inner thighs, her most intimate place…building inside her like a fleeting promise that she had to grab on to before it was taken away from her, before it vanished into thin air. Opening her eyes, she saw him staring at her, solemn and unsmiling, but exuding enough sexual chemistry to decimate an entire country.

'You leave tomorrow, Zahir.' Leaning towards him, she placed her hands on his shoulders, running them over the rough wool of the thick army jumper he was wearing. She loved the feel of him, the strength of the muscles, the way the thick column of his corded neck carried the pulse of his veins. 'I won't see you again before the wedding.'

'No.' His voice rumbled, deep and low, between them.

'If you wanted to make love to me…' she hesitated, trying very hard to control herself '…beforehand—now, even, I mean—I wouldn't object.'

'Of course you wouldn't.

Anna gasped at his chauvinistic attitude. But challenging it was going to be difficult when her body was still leaning in to him, inviting him, betraying her in the most obvious way.

'Are you so sure of yourself that you think you can have any woman of your choosing?'

'We are not talking about any woman. We are talking about my fiancée. You.' He lowered his mouth, his breath fanning across her face.

Anna swallowed. 'And that makes your conceit acceptable, does it?'

'Acceptable, inevitable, call it whatever you like.' His hand strayed to her neck, pushing aside the curtain of hair. 'And as for having no say in the matter…' Now his mouth was on her skin, the drag of his lips following the graceful sweep of her neck down to the hollow between her collarbone, muffling his words. 'You and I both know that you're desperate for me to make love to you.'

'That is very…' With her head thrown back to allow him more access to her throat, to make sure he had no excuse to stop lavishing this glorious attention on her neck, words were surprisingly hard to formulate. 'Ungallant.'

This produced a harsh laugh. 'I have never claimed to be gallant. Nor would you expect me to be. And, right now, I suspect gallantry is the last thing on your mind.' He raised his head his eyes drilling into her soul. 'Tell me, Annalina, which would you rather—a polite request to allow me access to your breasts, or an order that you remove your jumper?'

Anna gasped, the thrill of his audacious demand immediately shrivelling her nipples, producing a heavy ache in her breasts that rapidly spread throughout her body. It was outrageous, preposterous, that he should order her to strip.

'I thought as much.' Her second of silence was met with a growl of approval. 'Do it now, Annalina. Take off your jumper.'

She stared back at him, dumbfounded by the way this had suddenly turned around. How her tentative attempt to initiate lovemaking had resulted in an order to obey.

But still her fingers strayed to the bottom of her woollen jumper and she found herself pulling it up over her head, taking the tee-shirt underneath with it, until she was stripped down to her bra, her naked skin gleaming in the firelight.

'Very good.' Zahir's eyes travelled over her, his eyelids heavy, dark lashes flickering. Anna heard him swallow. 'Now, stay still.'

Raising both hands, he held them in front of her, their span so large, their skin so dark, as they hovered over the lacy white material of her bra. They were shaking, Anna realised. She was making the hands of this warrior man shake. Slowly they closed over her breasts, the heat of them searing into her, roaring through every part of her, right down to her fingertips that prickled by her side. And when his fingers traced where the swell of one of her breasts met the lacy fabric, dipping into the hollow of her cleavage before moving to explore the other, she thought she would combust with the agony and the ecstasy of it.

'Remove your bra.'

Reaching behind her, Anna did as she was told, any pretence of denying him or regaining control vanishing on the tidal wave of lust. As the bra fell to the floor, she kept her eyes fixed on Zahir's face, determined that she should see, as well as feel, his every reaction. He let out a guttural growl that arched her back, pushing her breasts towards him, inviting him to take her.

And take her he did. Cupping her naked breasts, one in each hand, he touched her hardened nipples with the pads of his thumbs, starting a rhythmic circular movement that had her writhing in front of him. Then, lowering his head, he took one nipple in his mouth, his breath scorching against her as he slathered her with hot, wet saliva before moving to the puckered peak, teasing his tongue against it with a slow, drugging forcefulness.

Anna groaned, her body on fire, dampness pooling between her legs, her skinny jeans suddenly unbearably tight, horribly uncomfortable. She wanted to take them off—bizarrely she wanted Zahir to tell her to take them off. But first she needed him to attend to her other breast before she died of longing.

A ragged sigh escaped her when he did just that, his attention to her second breast no more hurried, no less glorious. Anna plunged her fingers into his hair, pulling him closer to increase the pressure, to hold herself steady. She stared down, her eyes glazed, trance-like, as she watched his head rock against her, his mouth still working its incredible magic. And when he stopped, pulling away, ordering her to remove her jeans, she had no hesitation, falling over herself to stand up, undo the buttons and tug them down, cursing as they clung to her ankles and standing, first on one wobbly leg and then the other, as she pulled them inside out to get them off, ending up all but falling into Zahir's lap.

Strong arms encircled her, adjusting her position so that he held her, straddled across him, taking a second simply to look at her, his eyes raking over her like hot coals. She was acutely aware that she was virtually naked, whereas he was still fully dressed in rugged outdoor clothes, but for some reason this only increased her rabid desire. The scratch of his rough woollen jumper against her bare skin, the graze of the zips on the pockets of his cargo pants beneath her thighs, was something else, something so thrillingly erotic, that Anna couldn't hold back a squeak of surprise.

Zahir's erection, the enormous, rock-hard length of it, was like a rod of steel positioned between her buttocks, pulsing against her from behind. She tried to turn, to lift herself off so that she could find the zipper of his fly, her trembling fingers longing to yank it down, to release him so that she could see for herself, *feel* for herself, this extraordinary phenomenon. But Zahir held her firm, his hands around her waist gripping her so tightly that she could only move where he positioned her, which was squarely down on his lap again. She squirmed provocatively against him, the only small movement she could make. But even that was not allowed, as with a low growl Zahir lifted her up, the small space between them suddenly feeling like a yawning cavern of rejection, before he adjusted his position and sat her back down on him.

'Do not move.' The words roared softly into her ear from behind and Anna could only nod her acceptance as she felt one hand release her waist and move round to her front, where it trailed down over her clenching stomach muscles and slipped silently under the front of her skimpy lace knickers. The shock halted her breath, setting up a tremble that she couldn't tell whether was from inside her, or out, or both. She found herself desperately hoping that this didn't count as moving because she couldn't bear to disobey him now—not if it meant he was going to stop what he was doing. Gingerly tipping back her head, she rested it against the ridge of his collarbone, relieved when he seemed happy with this.

'That's right.'

His fingers brushed over her until they met the damp, throbbing centre of her core. Anna waited, poised on the brink of delirium, as one finger parted her sensitive folds, then slid into her with a slow but a deliberately controlled movement that shook her whole body from top to toe.

'Open your legs.'

The voice behind her commanded and Anna obeyed, parting her thighs, amazed that she had any control over any part of herself.

'Now, stop. Stay like that.'

It was like asking a jelly to stop wobbling, but Anna did the best she could, and with her head pressed hard back against his shoulder she screwed her eyes shut. Drawing in a breath, she waited, ready to give herself over to him completely, to do with her whatever he saw fit.

It was the most glorious, astonishing, explosion of mind-altering sensations. As his finger moved inside her, it rubbed against the swollen nub of her clitoris until he was just there, in that one spot, stroking it again and again with a pressure that could never be too much and never be enough. With the agonisingly pleasurable sensation swelling and swelling inside her, it felt as if her whole world had distilled into this moment, this momentous feeling. She would trade her entire life for the concentrated pleasure of this building ecstasy.

But trying to stay still was an impossibility. Even with the weight of Zahir's arm diagonally across her body she couldn't help writhing and bucking.

With his breath hot in her ear, the rock-hard swell of him beneath her buttocks, there was no way she could stop her legs from parting further, her back from arching against him, her bottom from pressing down into him. And as he continued his glorious attentions the pressure built more and more until what had seemed just tantalisingly out of reach was suddenly there upon her, crashing over her, carrying her with it. And, as that wave subsided and Zahir continued to touch her, another one followed, just as intense, then another and another, until Anna thought the moment might never end and that she had left the real world for ever.

But finally his hand stilled and slowly, slowly the feelings started to subside, sending sharp twitches through her body as reminders of what she had just experienced. Anna opened her eyes to see him staring down at her.

She looked so beautiful. Never had Zahir witnessed such beauty, such wild abandonment. Removing his arm, he released her body, moving her off his lap so that he could stand up, rip off his clothes and devour her in the way that he had been so desperate to do for the past hour…for the past twenty-four hours… ever since he had first clapped eyes on her. He had told himself that he would wait until after they were married, that that would be the right thing to do. But now waiting was an impossibility. Now the right thing, the *only* thing, he could think of was to claim this beautiful young woman for his own. To take her now, for himself, to satisfy his immense carnal need in the only way possible. By having her beneath him and making love to her in a way that neither of them would ever, ever forget.

With his breath coming in harsh pants, his chest heaving beneath the sweater that he tugged over his head, he was down to his boxer shorts in seconds, his powerful erection straining against the black cotton fabric, swollen and painful with need. He knew Anna was watching his every move from the floor, and that only increased his fervour, fuelled the frantic craving that was coursing through him.

'Lie down.' He barked the order without knowing why he felt the need to be so domineering.

Primal lust roared in his ears as he watched Annalina do as she was told, stretching out on the animal-skin rug, her body so pale in the flickering light of the fire, so delicate, so desirable. Bending down beside her, he pulled the scrap of fabric that was her panties down and over her legs, screwing them into a ball in his hand. Then he removed his boxers with a forceful tug and straddled her body with his own, holding his weight above her with locked elbows on either side of her head. She seemed so fragile compared to him, so impossibly perfect, that for a moment he could only gaze down at her, the corded muscles in his arms rigidly holding him in place, defying the tremor that was rippling through the rest of his body.

'You want this, Annalina?' He ground out the words, suddenly needing to hear her consent before he allowed himself to take her, this most precious creature.

'Yes.' It was the smallest word, spoken in little more than a whisper, but it was enough. And when her hand snaked between them, tentatively feeling for his member, he closed his eyes against the ecstasy, lowering his elbows enough to reach her lips and seal their coupling with a searing kiss.

Lifting himself off her, he unscrewed his eyes to look down at her again. Her hand was circling his shaft and it was taking all of his control not to position himself and plunge right into her. His need was so great, unlike anything he had ever felt before, that his body was screaming at him just to do it, to take her as fast and furiously as he liked, anything to satisfy this infernal craving. But he knew he had to find some restraint. If Annalina was a virgin, which it seemed she was, he had to try to take it slowly, make sure she was ready, control the barbarian in him. Though if she carried on the way she was right now, her fingers exploring the length of him, caressing the swollen tip, his body was going to have severe trouble obeying his commands.

'Is this right?' Slowly her hand moved up and down.

Zahir let out a moan of assent. Frankly she could have done it any damned way she liked, could have done anything she wanted. He was past the point of being able to judge.

'I don't want to disappoint you.'

Disappoint him? That was not going to happen. He was sure about that. He moved one arm to cover her hand with his own, to position himself over her, to the place he so desperately needed to be able to enter her. His fingers strayed to find her, to part her in readiness, but then something made him hesitate. The catch in her voice, the slight tremor, suddenly permeated the lust-ridden fog of his mind and now he rapidly scanned her face for clues.

'What is it? You have changed your mind?' It killed him to ask but he had to be sure.

'No, it's not that.'

'What, then?' So he had been right—there was something.

'Nothing, really.' She removed her hand, bringing her arms around his back. But, as they skittered over the play of his muscles, their touch was as unconvincing as her words.

'Tell me, Annalina.'

'Well, it's just… I'm a bit nervous.' Her throat moved beneath the pale skin of her throat. 'I hadn't realised that you would be so…large.'

'And that's a problem?'

'I don't know. I suppose it could be. I mean, there was a problem with me and Henrik, and he wasn't anything like as big…'

Henrik. The mention of his name on her lips had the effect of pouring an icy waterfall over Zahir, at the same time as stirring a roaring tiger in his chest. Henrik. He knew what he'd like to do if he ever got his hands on that slimy creep of an individual. He couldn't bear to think of him touching Annalina at any time, ever. But he particularly couldn't bear to think of him now.

'But I think we should try.' Still she was

talking, seemingly oblivious to the cold rage sweeping through him, her voice nervous but determined in the now suffocating air of the cabin. 'Now—before we marry, I mean—to see if we can. I'm worried because of what happened with Henrik…'

'Henrik!' Zahir roared his name, making Annalina jump beneath him. 'Do you really think I want to hear about Henrik?' He moved his body off her, leaping to his feet, cursing the damned erection that refused to die, mocking him with its disobedient show of power. 'Do you really think I want to be compared to your failed lover?'

'Well, no, but… I just meant…' Annalina sat up, covering her chest with her arms, her blue eyes staring up at him, wide, frightened and beseeching.

'I know what you meant. You meant that I'm not the man that you were meant to marry, the man you wanted to marry. You meant that having sex with me was a chore that you were prepared to endure. Or maybe not.' Another thought tore through his tortured mind. 'Maybe you thought that if we weren't able to have sex, if you could prove that, you wouldn't have to marry me at all.'

'No, Zahir, you're wrong. You've got it all wrong.'

'Because, if so, you are going to be sorely disappointed. We will marry, as planned, and we will consummate our marriage on our wedding night. And believe me, Annalina, when we do, I will drive all thoughts of Henrik from your mind. Banish all thoughts of not being able, or not being ready, or whatever other pathetic excuses you seem to be toying with. For when we do make love, when it finally happens, you'll be thinking of nothing but me. Nothing but the way *I* am making you feel. And that, Annalina, is a promise.

CHAPTER NINE

FROM INSIDE THE chapel the organ music paused and Princess Annalina's grip on her bouquet tightened. As the strains of Wagner's *Wedding March* began she felt for her father's arm, slipping her own through the crook of it. This was it, then. There was no going back now.

Not that she had any choice. Beside her King Gustav stood rigidly to attention, his gaze fixed straight ahead. If he had any misgivings about handing over his only daughter to this warrior prince, then he wasn't letting it show. As far as he was concerned this wedding was a business deal, a means to an end, and his job was to deliver his daughter to her fate. And to make sure that this time nothing went wrong.

Sitting side by side in the vintage car taking them the short journey from the castle to the chapel on the Valduz estate, Anna had thought maybe this would be the moment her father would say something encouraging, comforting—she didn't really know what. Instead he had simply checked his watch a dozen times, tugged on the sleeves of his morning coat and looked distractedly out of the window at the cheering crowds that lined the route as they passed. And when her hand had reached for his he had looked at it in surprise before awkwardly patting it a couple of times and handing it back.

More than anything in the world right now, Anna wished that her mother could be here to give her a hug, to make everything better. But sadly wishes didn't come true, even for princesses, so instead she ended up blinking back the tears as she stared out of the window, forcing herself to smile and wave at the crowds brandishing their paper flags. But inside she had never felt more lost. More alone.

The chapel doors opened to reveal the stage set for the ceremony. And it was beautiful. This was the first wedding the chapel had seen since her parents' nuptials and no expense had been spared, though it didn't take a genius to work out where the money had come from. With a green-and-white theme, the ancient pews were festooned with alpine flowers, their scent mingling with the incense in the air. Huge arrangements of ivy and ferns were positioned at the top of the aisle and behind the altar at the end—somewhere that Anna couldn't look at just yet.

Because that was where Zahir would be standing. Waiting. That was where, in just a few short minutes from now, the ceremony would begin that would see her signing away her life, at least the only life she had ever known. Where she would hand herself over to this man, become his wife, move to his country, to all intents and purposes become his property to do with as he saw fit.

And Anna had been left in no doubt as to what that would entail, at least as far as the bedroom was concerned. It had been four weeks since that fateful evening in the log cabin, but the brutal memory of it would stay with her for ever—the way Zahir had taken her from wild ecstasy to the pit of misery before the aftershocks of delirium had even left her body. His rage when she had mentioned Henrik had been palpable, terrifying, a dark force that had shocked her with its vehemence, leaving her no chance to try and explain why she had said it, to justify herself. Instead she had hurried to pull on her clothes and followed him out into the night, the snow falling as he had unerringly led them back to where their vehicle was parked and sat beside her in stony silence as she had driven them back to the castle.

Zahir had returned to Nabatean the next morning and they hadn't seen each other since, any contact between them limited to perfunctory emails or the occasional phone call. But his parting words still clamoured in her head. *We will consummate our marriage on our wedding night.* It had sounded more like a threat than a promise, but that didn't stop it sending a thrill of tumult through Anna whenever she recalled it. Like now, for example. Because tonight was the night that Zahir would fulfil his prophecy.

But first she had a job to do. Glancing behind her, she forced a smile at her attendants, four little bridesmaids and two pageboys. The daughters and sons of foreign royalty she didn't even know, they were nevertheless taking their duties very seriously, meticulously arranging the train of Anna's beautiful lace wedding dress, the girls bossing the boys around, straightening their emerald-green sashes for them before clasping their posies to their chests, ready to begin.

The procession started, slowly making its way down the red carpet, the congregation turning to catch their first glimpse of the blushing bride, gasping at what they saw. Because Annalina looked stunning, every inch the fairy-tale princess about to marry her Prince Charming. She wore a white lace gown, the wide V neck leaving her collarbone bare to show off the diamond necklace that had belonged to her mother. With sheer lace sleeves and a nipped-in waist, it cascaded to the floor with metres of lace and tulle that rustled with every step. Every step that took her closer and closer to the towering, dark figure that stood with his back to her—rigid, unmoving, impossible to read.

Zahir Zahani. The man she knew so little of, but who was about to become her husband. The man whose hooded gaze burnt into her soul, whose harshly sculpted face haunted her very being. The man who somehow, terrifyingly, she seemed to have become totally obsessed with. Even during the weeks when they had been apart it had felt as if her every waking moment had been filled with the overpowering sense of him. And not just her waking moments. The force of his magnetism had invaded her dreams too, seeing her writhing around in her sleep, waking up gasping for air, her heart thumping in her chest as the erotic images slowly faded into the reality of the day.

Now she took her position beside Zahir, beside this immovable mountain of a man who still stared fixedly ahead. His immaculate tailored suit only accentuated the width of his back, the length of his legs, and when Anna risked a sideways glance she saw how stiffly he held his neck against the starched white collar of his dress shirt, how rigidly his jaw was clenched beneath the smooth, olive skin.

Next to him stood Rashid, who was to serve as best man. In contrast to Zahir's complete stillness he fidgeted, shifting his weight from foot to foot, smoothing his hands over the trousers of his suit. He shot Anna a cold glance and again she registered that same peculiar sense of unease.

And so the long ceremony began. The sonorous voice of the priest echoed around the vaulted ceiling of the chapel—a chapel full of honoured guests from around the world. But Anna was only aware of one man, so acutely aware that she thought she must shimmer with it, radiate an aura that was plain for all to see.

Somehow she managed to get through the service, the daze of hymns, prayers, readings and blessings, only seriously faltering once, when Zahir slipped the platinum wedding ring onto her finger. The sight of it there, looking so real, so *final*, sent her eyes flying to his face, searching for a crumb of comfort, some sort of affirmation that they were doing the right thing. But all she saw was the same closed, dark expression that refused to give anything away.

Finally the organ struck up for the last time and the bride and groom made their way back up the aisle as man and wife. As they stepped outside, they were met with a loud roar from the crowd and a barrage of flashing cameras. It seemed thousands of people had gathered to be a part of this special day, braving hours of standing in the cold to catch a glimpse of their princess and her new husband. A short distance away, the car was waiting to take them back to the castle for the wedding breakfast, but first Anna was going to spend a few minutes chatting to the crowd. They deserved that, at least. Walking over to the barrier, she bent down to accept a posy of flowers from a young child, smiling at the sight of his chubby little cheeks red from the cold. The crowd roared louder and suddenly arms were reaching out everywhere, bunches of flowers thrust at them, cameras and phones held out to capture the moment.

'We need to get into the car, Annalina.' Zahir was right behind her, whispering harshly into her ear.

'All in good time.' She politely accepted another bunch of flowers. 'First we need to acknowledge the kindness of these people who have been hanging around for hours waiting to congratulate us.' She could feel Zahir's displeasure radiating from him in waves but she didn't care. They weren't in Nabatean now. This was her country and she was going to set the rules.

She continued to smile into the crowd, accepting armfuls of flowers that she then passed to a couple of burly men who had appeared behind them. She noticed they shot a startled glance at Zahir. 'Why don't you go and talk to the people over there?' She gestured to the barrier on the other side.

'Because this is not on the schedule, that's why.'

'So what? Life doesn't always have to run to a schedule.' She passed more flowers back to the minders, enjoying herself now, especially the sight of these burly men wreathed in blooms. 'You need to loosen up a bit, accept that this is the way things are done here.'

But Zahir showed no signs of loosening up. Instead he continued to move her forward by the sheer wall of his presence, so close behind her that his barely repressed ire bound them together. Anna turned her head, hissing the words past her smile: 'You might at least try and look as if you're happy.'

'This isn't about being happy.' No, of course it wasn't. How foolish of Anna to forget for a moment. 'Schedules are there for a reason. And impromptu *walkabouts* provide the ideal chance for a terrorist to strike.'

'This is Dorrada, Zahir.' Still she persisted. 'We don't have any terrorists.'

They had reached the car now, Zahir having to duck his head to get in to this ancient vehicle that had once been her father's pride and joy. He seemed far too big for it, caged in by it, as the doors closed behind them, muffling the cheers of the crowd.

'May I remind you that you are now married to me, Annalina? To Prince Zahir of Nabatean?' He turned to face her, his eyes as black as stone. 'And *we* do. From now on, you will treat security with the respect it deserves. Otherwise, you may not live to regret it.'

Zahir's eyes strayed across the crowded ballroom yet again, searching out Annalina. She wasn't difficult to find. Still wearing her wedding dress, she was by far the most beautiful woman in the room without exception, moving amongst the guests with practised ease, charming them with her grace and beauty, occasionally taking to the floor to be whisked around by some daring young buck or crusty old dignitary.

Zahir didn't dance. Never had he seen the need. But tonight he found himself wishing that he did, that he could have parted the crowd on the dance floor, firmly tapped on the shoulder whichever interloper it was at the time and removed Annalina from his clutches. Other men touching his bride did not sit well with him. More than that, it spread a hot tide of possessiveness through him, the like of which he had never known before. It was something he knew he had to keep in check.

At least until tonight, when he would have Annalina in his bed. Then she would be all his, in every sense of the word. It was that thought that had got him through today: the long-drawn-out ceremony, the tedious wedding breakfast and now this irksome ball that it appeared would never come to an end. His tolerance and patience had been severely tested, neither being qualities that he had in abundance. But the day was finally drawing to a close, the waiting nearly over. And as the time approached when at last they would be together, alone, so the thrum of awareness increased, spreading through him, until it was no longer a thrum but a thudding, pounding urge that held his body taut, rang in his ears.

From across the other side of the room Annalina looked up, meeting his gaze, a gaze which he knew he had held for too long, that was in danger of betraying him with its intensity. She angled her head, something approaching a smile playing across her lips, her eyes deliberately holding his, refusing to look away.

God, she was beautiful. A fresh wave of lust

washed over him, tightening the fit of his tailored trousers. She might be all demure decorum now but tonight he would have those restrained lips screaming his name in pleasure, those searching eyes screwed shut against the delirium of his touch, his heated thrust. Bringing her to orgasm that night in the log cabin had been the single most erotic experience of his life. But the experience had ended badly—seeing him consumed with rage, fighting to maintain his composure, dangerously close to losing it. This was what Annalina did to him. She stirred up emotions that were totally uncalled for. Awoke the warrior in him when the situation called for restraint and respect—not pumping testosterone and raging hormones.

As the supreme leader of the army of Nabatean, Zahir had seen some terrible things, had done some terrible things, that still had the power to haunt him when he closed his eyes against the night. But that was war, the most brutal savagery imaginable, man turning on his fellow man. It had been a hideous, necessary evil but he was vindicated by the fact that Nabatean was now a successful, independent country, free from the oppression and tyranny of its war-mongering neighbour. Many would say that Zahir should be extremely proud of his achievements. That he had accomplished what no man had ever thought possible. But, despite his pride in his country, Zahir would never be able to accept praise for his victory, let alone celebrate it. Not when his parents had paid for his success with their lives.

He had learned his lesson in the most painful way possible. Never again would he allow himself the luxury of such gratification, no matter for how brief a period of time. Self-indulgent pleasure was to be avoided at all costs. He just needed to remember that when he was around Annalina.

Not that his feelings for her were all about pleasure, far from it. Annalina stirred up extremes of emotions that were as threatening as they were mystifying.

For a slightly built young woman, weighing, he would estimate, little more than eight stone, this was extremely perplexing. Even if she'd been a trained assassin, armed to the teeth, he knew he would have no trouble overpowering her, throwing her to the ground, dispatching her if necessary. But she wasn't a trained assassin and she wasn't armed, at least, not with a recognisable weapon. She was no threat. So why did his body insist that she was, firing the blood through his veins as if he had stepped into an ambush, had a blade at his throat?

Because Annalina's weapons were of a different kind. Ice-blue eyes that flashed with a mystery all of their own. Plump lips, pert breasts, hair that tumbled over her shoulders… curves that begged to be stroked. These were her weapons. And Zahir was beginning to realise that they were more lethal than any he had come across before. They consumed his mind, invaded his consciousness, provoking feelings of anger, lust and a desperate need that had only increased in the weeks they had been apart. And there was another emotion, one he had never experienced before. *Jealousy.* The thought of Annalina with another man, past or present, innocent or not, gripped him hard enough to paralyse his whole body. It frightened him with its force, weakened him with its power.

Forcing himself to relax, he leant against a pillar festooned with winter foliage, flexing his fingers, half-closing his eyes. Eyes that still followed Annalina as she started talking to another guest—that narrowed further when he saw the man taking her hand in his, raising it to his lips, holding it there longer than was strictly necessary. He sucked in a breath. *Control yourself, Zahir. And find enough patience for another hour.* When they finally did come together, it would be all the sweeter for the wait.

He was glad now that they hadn't had sex that night in the cabin. At the time it had only been blind rage that had stopped him. But now he knew the timing hadn't been right. He had wanted her—God how he had wanted her! But deep down had he felt uneasy about despoiling such an exquisite creature? Felt unworthy, even? Now Annalina was his bride, his wife. Now he could legitimately claim her. And any unusually sensitive worries he might have had, any hesitancy about his rights or his responsibilities, had long since vanished in a sea of carnal craving.

Shouldering himself away from the pillar, he decided to go outside in search of some fresh air. He needed to cool himself down.

It was a beautiful night, crisp and clear, with a full moon shining on the virgin snow. Zahir paused to take in the view, the town of Valduz spread out in the valley below twinkling prettily, the mountains all around them soaring into the night sky. He set off around the side of the castle, his footprints sinking deep into the crunchy snow, breathing in deeply to relish the cold air that scoured his lungs. But then he stopped, his senses on high alert. Someone else was out here. He could hear the huff of their breath, a sort of shuffling noise, a mumbled voice.

Zahir moved stealthily forward, tracking the sound like the trained killer that he was. Now he could make out the shape of man leaning against the wall of the castle, see the glow of a cigarette burn more brightly as he took a deep drag before flicking it away into the snow. He watched as the figure raised a bottle to his lips—whisky, if Zahir had to guess—glugging from it greedily then wiping the back of his hand across his mouth before staggering a couple of steps sideways, then back again. The mumbling was him talking to himself. There was no one else was around. He was clearly very drunk.

Zahir stepped out of the shadows.

'I think you've had enough of this.' Removing the bottle from the man's grasp, Zahir flung it behind him.

'Hey!' Lunging forward, the man peered at him with glassy-eyed aggression. 'What the hell do you think you're doing?'

Zahir silently positioned himself in front of this creature, squaring his chest, towering over him. He wasn't looking for a fight, but neither was he going to let this guy drink himself into oblivion. Not here, at his wedding party.

'You have no right to…' Squinting up at Zahir, the man suddenly stopped. 'Well, look who it is. The mighty desert Prince.' A sneer twisted his thin lips. 'What brings you out here? Trying to escape already?'

Zahir's fists balled by his sides. This individual was seriously asking for a punch.

'You don't know who I am, do you?' Pushing himself unsteadily off the wall, he straightened up, holding Zahir's gaze, emboldened by the alcohol or stupidity, or both. 'Allow me to introduce myself. Prince Henrik of Ebsberg.' He extended a limp arm. 'Delighted to meet you.'

Blood roared in Zahir's ears, raging through his body, turning his muscles to stone. So this was the revolting individual who had once been engaged to Annalina. His fists by his sides flexed, then balled again, his nails digging into his palms.

'Ha.' With a dismissive laugh, Henrik withdrew his hand, folding his arms over his chest. 'So my name's familiar to you, then.' He put his head on one side, the sneer still curving his lips. 'You may not want to shake my hand, old chap, but perhaps you will accept my heartfelt commiserations instead. You have my deepest sympathies.'

A growl erupted from somewhere deep inside Zahir as he adjusted his stance, planting his feet further apart. 'And just what do you mean by that?'

'Oh, dear.' With a giggle, Henrik moved his

hand to his mouth. 'Don't tell me you don't know. This is *so* much worse than I thought.'

'Don't know what?' Zahir ground out the question, more as a diversionary tactic to stop his hands from travelling to this man's throat rather than because he wanted an answer.

'About your new bride. I'm sorry to be the bearer of bad news, but Princess Annalina is not only as pure as the driven snow, she's as frozen as it.' Misinterpreting Zahir's thunderous silence, Henrik warmed to his theme. 'Yes, it's true. Beneath that pretty exterior there lies nothing but a block of ice.'

'Hold your tongue.' Zahir bent down, his face just inches away from his prey. 'You will not speak of my wife in such a way. Not if you know what's good for you.'

'Why not?' Henrik blithely carried on. 'I'm only telling you the truth. Annalina is the original ice maiden. You will get no satisfaction from her. Take it from me. I should know. I've been there.'

Unbidden, Zahir's hands flew to Henrik's throat, grasping a handful of shirt and lifting his feet clean off the ground. The fury that engulfed him was so strong he could taste it, feel it rising up his throat, burning behind his eyes. The thought that this man had even touched Annalina was enough for Zahir to wish upon him the most slow and painful death. But to brag about it. To speak of her in that hideously insulting manner… Death would be too good for him.

He looked down at Henrik, now squirming in his grasp. Then, taking a deep breath, he let him go, watching as he fell to his knees before scrabbling to stand upright again.

'Tut, tut.' Brushing the snow from his hands, Henrik staggered a couple of steps away. 'It's not my fault that you've married a dud, Zahani. You should have taken a leaf out of my book and had the sense to try her out first. I had a lucky escape. But you, my friend, have been duped.'

'Why, you little…' Raging fury had all but closed Zahir's throat, grinding his words to a low snarl. 'Get out of my sight while you can still walk.'

'Very well. But it won't change anything. The fact is, pretty Annalina is frigid. If it's any consolation, I had no idea either—not until she was in my bed, until she was under me, until it came to the actual point of—'

Crack. Zahir's fist connected with Henrik's nose, making a noise like the fall of a branch in the forest. With this vilest of creatures now splayed at his feet, his first thought was of satisfaction, that he had finally silenced his revolting words. But rampant fury was still pumping through his body, the temptation to finish what he had started holding him taut, tensing his muscles, grinding his jaw. He looked down at Henrik, who was whimpering pathetically, blood pouring from his nose.

'Get up.' He realised he wasn't done with him yet. He wanted him on his feet again, wanted him to fight back, to give him the opportunity to have another swipe at him. But Henrik only moaned. 'I said, get up.' Bending down, Zahir lifted him by the scruff of the neck again, holding him before him like a rag doll. 'Now put your fists up. Fight like a man.'

'Please, no.' Henrik raised a hand, but only to touch his damaged nose, recoiling in horror when it came away covered in blood. 'Let me go. I don't want to fight.'

'I bet you don't.' Zahir set him down again, watching Henrik's knees buckle in the struggle to keep him upright. 'Call yourself a man, *Prince Henrik of Ebsberg*?' He spat out the name with utter revulsion. 'You are nothing more than a pathetic piece of scum, a vile and despicable low life. And if I ever hear you so much as utter Princess Annalina's name, let alone defile her character as you have just done, you will not live to tell the tale. Is that understood?'

Henrik nodded and Zahir turned away, taking several steps, inhaling deeply as he did so, trying to purge himself of this man. He was ten or twelve feet away when Henrik called after him.

'So it's true what they say about you.'

Zahir froze, then slowly turned around.

'You really *are* an animal. The Beast of Nabatean.' His words slurred into one another. 'You do know that's what they call you, don't you?' He started to giggle idiotically. 'Despite your marriage, Europe will never accept you. So you see, you and Annalina, it's all been for nothing. Beauty and the Beast—you deserve each other.'

The space between them was closed in an instant, even though Henrik was backing away as fast as his collapsing legs would let him.

Zahir's fist connected with Henrik's face again—this time it was his jaw. And, when he fell to the snow again, this time there was no getting up.

CHAPTER TEN

CLOSING THE DOOR, Anna leant back against it and looked around. The room was empty. She was the first to arrive. Swallowing down the jittery disappointment, she drew in a deep breath. It was fine. She would have time to prepare herself before Zahir came to her. And when he did she would be ready. They would make love and everything would be wonderful. This was the night that finally, please God, she would lose not only her virginity but the terrible stigma that had haunted her for so long.

The room assigned to the newlyweds had been dressed for the occasion. Rugs were scattered over the polished wooden floor, heavy curtains pulled against the freezing night, an enormous tapestry adorning one stone wall. A fire roared in the grate and that, along with the guttering candles in the iron chandelier overhead, provided the only light.

Anna moved over to the bed. Centuries old,

the oak construction was raised off the floor by a stepped platform, with four columns to support the heavy square-panelled canopy. Drapes were tied back to reveal the sumptuous bedding, piles of pillows and embroidered silk throws. She sat on the edge, sinking down into the soft mattress, then ran her fingers over the coverlet, her eyes immediately drawn to the wedding ring on her finger. So it was true—she really had married her dashing Arabian prince. There was her evidence.

Being reunited with Zahir today, seeing him again in all his gorgeously taut, olive-skinned flesh, had been both wonderful and agonising. Because it had confirmed what she already knew in her heart. That Zahir was like a drug to her, a dangerous addiction that had invaded her cells to the point where she found she craved him, ached for him. But, just like an addiction, she knew she had to face up to it in order to be able to control it.

Because giving in to her weakness, letting it take over, control her, would be her undoing. Over the years she had learnt how protect herself, to hide her emotional vulnerability. She had had to. Because there had been precious little love in her life since her mother had died. She didn't blame her father for his coldness. It wasn't his fault that he couldn't love her the way she wanted him to. It was hers. And when she'd tried to please him—agreeing to marry Henrik, for example—she'd ended up just making things worse. The broken engagement, the dreadful shame, the *crippling humiliation* only served to compound her feelings of lack of self-worth. She feared she wasn't capable of being loved, in any sense of the word. And for that reason she had to protect her own heart. She had to be very, very careful.

She thought back over the day she and Zahir had just shared, their wedding day. She had been so aware of his presence—every second of every hour—that it had felt almost like a physical pain. Standing rigidly beside her during the ceremony, silently consuming his meal next to her at the wedding breakfast or scowling across at her during the ball, her skin had prickled from the sense of him, the hairs on the back of her neck standing on end, her nerve endings tingling.

But then towards the end of the evening something had happened, something telling—thrilling. Their eyes had met across the ballroom and they had shared a look, an understanding. Zahir's gaze had scorched a path between them, his hooded, mesmerising eyes spelling out exactly what was on his mind. *Hunger and desire*. It had been a look of such unconscious seduction, such inevitability, that it had weakened her knees, caught the breath in her throat. Zahir wanted her. She was sure of that. And she wanted him too, more than she could ever have imagined wanting any man, *ever.* That didn't mean she could let down her guard—in fact now she would need to protect herself more than ever. But it did mean that the time was right. They were both ready.

So when Zahir had turned and left the ballroom Anna had prepared to leave too. Heart thumping, she had made her excuses to her guests, hurrying her goodbyes in her rush to follow him, to be with him. Because tonight was the night that Zahir would make love to her. And this time she was determined that everything would be all right.

Now she smoothed her hands over the folds of her wedding dress. All day long she had had visions of Zahir undressing her, his fingers impatiently tugging at the fiddly buttons, pulling the fine lace over her shoulders, watching the dress fall to the ground.

Well, maybe she would save him the bother. Standing up, she twisted behind her and undid the top buttons as best she could then wriggled out of the dress and placed it carefully over the back of a chair. Next she pulled out the clips that held up her hair, undoing the braids and threading her fingers through to release them until her hair tumbled over her shoulders. She looked down at herself. At the white lace bra and panties, the white silk stockings that revealed several inches of bare skin at the top of her thighs. Goosebumps skittered over her. Away from the fire, the room felt cold. But inside Anna already burned for Zahir's touch, her body clenching at the thought of it. She wanted him so badly.

On impulse she pulled back the covers and got into bed, squirming into the sheets. Would it please Zahir to come across her like this—still in her underwear? She had no idea. She had no sexual experiences to draw on. All she knew was that, lying here semi-naked like this, she felt as sexy as hell, and that had to be a good place to start. Her hand strayed to her panties, to the soft mound of hair beneath. Tentatively her fingers slipped under the skimpy fabric, finding their way to her intimate folds. She was damp, already very aroused. Slowly, slowly, she started to gently rub herself, prepare herself for Zahir, for what was to come. Letting out a sigh, she rested her head back against the pillow and closed her eyes.

A sudden noise snapped them open again—the wail of an ambulance siren. Pushing herself up to sitting, Anna rubbed her eyes. She hoped a guest hadn't been taken ill. What time was it? And where was Zahir? She noticed that the fire was burning low in the grate—she must have fallen asleep. Checking her watch, she realised that nearly an hour had passed since she had come to the bridal suite. More than enough time for Zahir to have joined her.

A terrible fear gripped her heart. Pulling back the covers, she tugged a throw off the bed and wrapped it around her, her body already starting to shake. She moved over to the fireplace, bending to pick up a log and throw it onto the glowing embers, watching the shower of sparks. Then, settling into a low chair, she drew up her knees and pulled the throw around her, her mind racing in all directions.

Maybe he had been waylaid. Perhaps one of the guests, one of the many foreign dignitaries that he had been conversing with all day, had suggested they talked business before he retired to bed.

Maybe he hadn't been able to find the right room. Maybe he was wandering around the castle right now, opening doors, calling her name. Although it was pushing it to think that a man who could navigate the vastness of the desert by the stars alone would have trouble finding his way to the marital bed.

Or maybe he had been taken ill. The ambulance she had heard just now might be coming to whisk him to hospital because he'd been struck down with some mystery ailment. But that seemed equally unlikely. It was impossible to believe that Zahir Zahani had ever had a day's sickness in his life.

Which only left one more possibility—the most painful one of all. *He wasn't coming.* She must have misinterpreted the look he had given her in the ballroom—or, worse, she had imagined it completely. Like a starving dog, she had gobbled up the scrap being thrown to her, convinced that it was the start of a feast, that her hunger would finally be satisfied. But she had been wrong. And now, like a useless cur, she had been abandoned.

As she stared into the flames that were starting to leap into life, she felt the tears blocking her throat. Now the real reason Zahir wasn't here was all too obvious.

He didn't want her. Now he knew the truth, that she was frigid, incapable of ever being able to satisfy him, he had no use for her. *Somehow this time, without even having got Zahir to her bed, she had managed to fail yet again.*

Zahir stared at the man sprawled at his feet. Anger was still coursing through him, clenching his fists and his teeth, holding every muscle rigid in his body.

Bending down, he grabbed hold of Henrik's shoulder and roughly turned him over, hearing him moan as he did so. Blood stained the snow where his face had been, seeping into the icy imprint. His face was a mess with blood flowing from his nose and mouth, his lip split and swelling. Judging from the angle of his jaw, it was definitely dislocated.

Zahir let out a long, slow breath, releasing the last of his rage into the darkness of the night. *The Beast of Nabatean.* So that was how he was known in the West. And now he had just lived up to his name.

Well, so be it. He didn't give a damn. If European society wanted to look over their monocles, hide behind their simpering manners and call him a beast, then he would accept the title. Accept it with pride, in fact. For it was his strength, his fearlessness—and, yes, at times the brutality of his decisions—that had won his country their independence. He would value that over their delicate Western sensibilities a thousand times.

But Annalina…that was a different matter. Was that how she thought of him? Like some sort of beast or barbarian that fate had cruelly delivered to her door? To her bed? The thought struck him like a savage blow. Certainly he had done nothing to dispel the myth. He had never shown her the slightest care or consideration. Because he didn't know how. He was a military man, comfortable only with logic and detachment, proud of his nerves of steel. He could cope with any situation, no matter how horrific. Hadn't he demonstrated that with the way he had handled the slaughter of his parents? A situation that would have tested the strongest man. That had ripped his brother apart, both mentally and physically. But he had taken charge, dealt with the carnage the only way he knew how. By banishing his emotions, refusing to give in to any weakness and concentrating on finding the perpetrators. Then trying to minimise the repercussions for all concerned. He had never even let himself grieve. He couldn't afford to.

But the war was over now, and the military training that had held him in such good stead no longer applied. Now he found he didn't know how to behave. Now he was left wondering who the hell he was.

He looked down at his battered victim again. Beneath the anger he could feel another emotion pushing through—disgust. And not just for the man at his feet, although that was a palpable force. But disgust at himself too. Raising his hand, he saw the blood that stained his knuckles, knuckles that were swelling from the force of his punch.

He could have walked away. He *should* have walked away. But he couldn't do it, could he? He couldn't control himself. He was deserving of his title. A beast.

What he didn't deserve was the beautiful young woman he had married today. Who was expecting him in her bed tonight. Who no doubt was bracing herself, preparing to accept the fate that he had spelt out that night in the cabin. Not because she wanted to, but because she had no alternative other than to do as she was told. Zahir wanted her so badly, he had tried to justify his arrogant, dictatorial behaviour by telling himself it was her duty, not least because she was now his wife. But this wasn't about duty, no matter how much he tried to dress it up. It was about his carnal cravings. And there was no way he would allow himself to indulge them tonight. He had another man's blood on his hands. How could he even consider using these same hands to touch Annalina, to claim her for himself? He couldn't. It would be an insult to her beauty and to her innocence. Denying himself that pleasure would be his penance.

Henrik groaned again. He needed medical

attention—that much was obvious. Pulling his mobile phone out of his pocket, Zahir called for an ambulance, ending the conversation before the operator could ask him any more questions. They knew enough to come and patch him up, restore his pretty-boy good looks.

Throwing his victim one last look of revulsion, he turned away. Then, jamming his hands down into his pockets, he hunched his shoulders against the cold and began to walk. He didn't know where to and he didn't know how far. All he did know was that he had to get away from here, from this creature, from the castle, and from the desperate temptation to slide into bed next to the luscious body of his new bride.

CHAPTER ELEVEN

A SMALL RECEPTION party had lined up to welcome Prince Zahir and his new wife when they arrived back at Medira Palace. As Zahir swept them through the massive doors, Anna forced herself to smile at everyone, especially when she saw Lana and Layla, standing on tiptoes trying to get a better look at them. They looked so excited it made her want to cry.

Little more than twenty-four hours had passed since their marriage ceremony, since they had stood side by side in the chapel in Dorrada and made their vows. But it had been long enough to spell out just what sort of a marriage it would be. Hollow and empty and desperately lonely. Long enough to firmly dash any hopes she might have foolishly fostered that they could ever be a real couple, come together as husband and wife, as lovers.

It was also a marriage where she was going to have to be constantly on her guard, hide her true feelings from Zahir. Because to show him even a glimmer of what was in her heart would be emotional suicide. She could hardly bring herself to examine the insanity of her own feelings, let alone expose them to the cold and cruel claws of her husband.

Her wedding night had been miserably sad, plagued by fitful dreams and long periods of wakefulness in a bed that had seemed increasingly empty as the hours of darkness had dragged by. Forcing herself to go down to breakfast this morning had taken all the will power she possessed but she'd known she had to face Zahir sometime. Somehow she had to cover up her broken heart. But as it turned out she'd been met, not by her husband, but with a note presented on a silver salver and written in Zahir's bold hand, stating that she was to meet him at the airport in two hours' time. That they would be flying back to Nabatean without delay. And that was it. No explanation as to where he had been all night, where he was now. No apology or excuses of any kind.

Because, as far as Zahir was concerned, she didn't deserve any explanations. She was now his property—by dint of their marriage, he had effectively bought her, no matter how it had been dressed up with fancy ceremonies and profuse congratulations. Now she belonged to him, in the same way as a herd of camel or an Arabian stallion. Except she was of considerably less use. If she couldn't satisfy him in bed, couldn't give him an heir, then, other than the connection with Europe that came with her position, what purpose did she actually serve?

No doubt Zahir was wondering the same thing. No doubt that was the reason he hadn't come to her bed last night and the reason he had totally ignored her on the flight to Nabatean, preferring the company of his laptop instead. The reason why his mood was as black as thunder as he briskly moved past the reception party and headed straight down the maze of corridors that lead to his private quarters.

Anna stood in the echoing reception chamber and looked around her, breathing in the foreign air of this gilded cage. Here she was in her new role, her new life. And she had no idea what she was supposed to do with it.

Declining the offer of refreshments, she allowed herself to be shown to the suite of rooms that had been assigned to her and Zahir. The grand marital bedroom had a raised bed centre-stage, like some sort of mocking altar, and the only slightly less grand bedroom, which she was solemnly informed was her personal room, just served to increase her sense of isolation, filled her with misery. What sort of marriage needed separate bedrooms right from the off? Sadly, she already knew the answer to that.

Wandering downstairs again, she found herself in one of the many empty salons and sat down on a window seat that overlooked a verdant courtyard. Darkness had fallen, the night having arrived with indecent haste in this part of the world, and the courtyard was floodlit, the palm trees and the fountain illuminated with a ghostly orange glow.

Anna felt for her phone in her handbag. She needed a distraction to stop herself from bursting into tears or running screaming into the wilderness of the desert, or both. Clicking on the site of a national newspaper in Dorrada, she scrolled through the headlines until she found what she was looking for. Just as she had expected, there was extensive coverage of the wedding of Princess Annalina to Prince Zahir of Nabatean, gushing descriptions of the beautiful ceremony, the sumptuous banquet and the glittering ball that had followed. Other European papers hadn't stinted either, all showing the official photographs accompanied by the obligatory text describing the couple's happy day.

Anna studied the images. She and Zahir, standing side by side, her arm linked through his. She could see the tension in her face, that the smile was in danger of cracking. And Zahir, tall, commanding, looking impossibly handsome with his shoulders back and his head held high. But his expression was masked, closed, impossible to fathom, no matter how much Anna stared at it. She was left wondering just who this man was that she had married.

She was about to put her phone away when a headline on one of the sidebars caught her eye. The shot of a battered face, captured by a zoom lens, by the look of it, was accompanied by the headline: *Prince Henrik arrives at hospital with facial injuries.*

A cold dread swept over her. With a shaky hand, she clicked on the link.

Prince Henrik of Ebsberg was seen arriving at a Valduz hospital on the night of his ex-fiancée's wedding, sporting what appeared to be significant facial injuries. One can only speculate as to how he acquired them.

Prince Henrik is known to have attended the grand ball thrown to celebrate the marriage of Princess Annalina of Dorrada to Prince Zahir of Nabatean. Could it be that the two men came to blows over the beautiful blonde princess? If so, it would appear that Prince Zahir's reputa-

tion as a formidable opponent is fully justified. Neither Prince Henrik nor Prince Zahir was available for comment.

No! Anna's heart plummeted inside her. Had Zahir done this to Henrik? She didn't want to believe it but her gut was telling her it had to be him. Head spinning, she desperately tried to think up some other explanation, figure out what could possibly have happened.

As European royals, the King and Queen of Ebsberg had been present at the wedding but Anna had been thankful, at that point, to see that their son, Henrik, hadn't joined them. She had completely forgotten about him until much later at the ball when out of the corner of her eye she had seen him arrive, looking unsteady on his feet, as if he had already been drinking. Having absolutely no desire to speak to him, she had deliberately kept out of his way, relieved that the relatively late hour meant she could legitimately slip away before he could corner her. But had Zahir spoken to him? Deliberately sought him out? Had it always been his intention to beat up her ex-fiancé?

The barbaric thought made Anna feel physically sick. But there was only one way to find out if it was true.

Leaping to her feet, she set off to find Zahir,

pausing only briefly to try and get her bearings, to remember the way to his private quarters. With her pace quickening along with her temper, she flew along the echoing corridors, finally arriving at his door breathless and panting with anger. Rapping loudly on the panelling, she hurtled in without waiting for a reply.

'What is the meaning of this?' She advanced towards him, brandishing her phone before her like a weapon.

Rising from where he had been seated at a computer, Zahir met her head-on, towering before her. 'I could ask the same of you.' Deep-set eyes flashed dangerously black. 'I don't take kindly to being ambushed in my own study.'

'And I don't suppose Prince Henrik takes kindly to being beaten up by some vicious thug.' Trembling with animosity, Anna thrust the phone in his face. Taking it from her, Zahir gave it a cursory glance before tossing it back. Anna fumbled to catch it. 'Well? What do you have to say?' She could feel the hysteria rising in the face of his silence and the mounting realisation that she was right—Zahir had assaulted Henrik. 'Do you know about this? Did you *do* this?'

'I fail to see that this is any of your concern.'

'Not my concern?' Her voice screeched with incredulity. 'How can you say that? It's obvi-

ous that you attacked Henrik because of his association with me!'

'Trust me, there are any number of reasons I could have hit that creature.'

'So you admit it, then? You did assault Henrik?'

Zahir shrugged and his dismissive gesture only served to pour more fuel onto Anna's fury.

'And that's it? That's all you have to say on the matter?' She threw back her head so he couldn't escape her livid gaze. 'Aren't you at least going to offer some explanation, show some concern for what you've done?'

'I think you're showing enough concern for both of us.'

The air crackled between them, stirring the shadows of this cave-like room.

'What do you mean by that?'

'Some might say that you are unduly concerned about someone you should no longer have any attachment to.'

'Don't be ridiculous.'

'That you are displaying the behaviour of someone who still has feelings for this man.'

'No…'

'Are you regretting the past? Is that what it is? Do you wish you were married to him instead of me?'

'No, no, it's not that at all.'

'Isn't it, Annalina? Are you sure? You've told me yourself that it was Henrik who broke off your engagement. You still want him, don't you? That's the reason you are displaying such irrational behaviour.'

Irrational behaviour? Anna's eyes glittered back at him like shards of glass. She knew what he was doing: he was trying to make out that she was overreacting—that, even though he was the one who had committed the crime, she was the one who should be examining her motives. Well, she wasn't having it. Positioning herself squarely in front of him, she clenched her teeth, ready to fire at him with both barrels.

'Has it ever occurred to you, Zahir…' she swallowed audibly '…that I may be displaying the behaviour of someone who's worried that they have married a monster?'

A terrible silence fell between them. For a moment neither of them moved, their eyes locked in a lethal clash that Anna couldn't break but that tore into her soul. She could hear the roar of blood in her ears, feel the heavy thud of her heartbeat, but she was paralysed, Zahir's painfully piercing black stare holding her captive as surely as if she'd been nailed to the ground.

'And that's what you think, is it?' His voice was lethally low, barely more than a murmur.

But it carried the weight of the loudest scream. 'You think that I am a monster?'

'I didn't actually say that.'

'Well, you are not alone. The Beast of Nabatean—isn't that what they call me?'

'No, I mean…'

'Don't bother to try and deny it. I know full well how the European bourgeoisie perceive me.'

'But not me, Zahir. I would never call you such a thing.' Anna had heard the insulting title—of course she had—but a loathing of prejudice and bigotry, and maybe a smattering of fear, had made her dismiss it. Until now. 'This isn't about what other people call you. And it's nothing to do with how I feel about Henrik. It's about you going around beating people up.'

'And you think that's what I do?'

'Well, what am I supposed to think?'

'I'd like you to leave now.' He turned away and she was suddenly presented with the impenetrable wall of his back.

'What? No!' Horrified, she reached forward, her fingers clawing at the fabric of his shirt. 'I'm not going until we have discussed this, until you have heard me out.'

'I *said* I want you to leave.'

'And if I refuse?'

'Who knows what might happen, Annalina? How I might react.' Swinging round, he closed the space between them with a single step, then towered over her, his fixed gaze as black as a raven's wing. 'Are you prepared to take that risk? Are you prepared to incur the wrath of such a monster as me?' His words were clearly designed to intimidate her and it was working, at least to start with, Anna's throat drying, her hands shaking from the sheer force of his might.

But as she continued to stare at him a different reaction started to seep in. Suddenly her breasts felt heavy, her nipples contracting, her belly clenching with a fierceness that rippled down to her core, holding it tight in its grip. Suddenly her whole body was alive to him. And it was nothing to do with fear.

She watched as his pupils dilated, her own doing the same in response. So he felt it too. Anger still pulsed between them but now it was laced with hunger, a carnal craving that was growing more powerful with each suspenseful second.

She forced herself to swallow. How could she want this man so badly? It didn't make any sense. How could she have given her heart to a man capable of such savagery? Capable of hurting her so badly? The wounds inflicted on their wedding night, still raw and bleeding, were a painful testament to that. But a monster? No. Arrogant, insufferable, formidable… Anna could reel off a list of his shortcomings. But loyal too and fiercely protective. She had seen the way he was with his brother, glimpsed the burden of pain and suffering caused by his parents' tragic deaths before he had pulled down the shutters and pushed her away. She had heard the pride in his voice whenever he spoke of his country. No, Zahir was no monster.

'Well?' He bit out the word but there was an edge to his voice that betrayed him, angered him. He extended his arm, roughly clasping the back of her head, threading his fingers through her hair to bring her closer to him. 'I'm still waiting for your answer.'

His breath was hot on her face and Anna's tongue darted to wet her lips. 'I'm still here, aren't I?'

'So it would seem.' He moved fractionally closer until their bodies were touching. Heat roared between them, the unmistakable stirring beneath Zahir's trousers making Anna tremble violently. 'But what does that tell me? That you don't think that I'm a monster? Or that right now you don't care?'

'I'm not frightened of you, Zahir, if that's what you mean.'

'Hmm. And yet you are shaking. Why is that, Annalina?'

'I d-don't know.'

'Maybe it's that you crave the beast in me.' He moved closer still, pressing the length of his body against her, all heat and flexed muscle, hard bones beneath tautly drawn flesh. And raw, potent, sexual energy.

'And if I do?'

'Then perhaps it is my duty to satisfy that craving.'

Finally his lips came down to claim hers with a punishing kiss that sucked the air from her lungs, pumped the blood wildly around her body. He plundered her mouth, his tongue seeking and taking, his breath feverishly hot as he panted into her. It was a kiss that left Anna reeling from its force, melting beneath its pressure. She gasped as he finally pulled away, feeling her lips engorging with blood before he was kissing her again, moving his hands to span the small of her back, pressing her firmly against his erection. Complete abandonment washed over her as the most gloriously erotic feeling took over, obliterating all thought. Other than that Zahir *had* to make love to her. *Now.*

When their lips finally pulled apart she worked her hands around his waist to the strip of bare skin between his shirt and the low-slung pants, feeling him buck satisfyingly beneath her touch. Easily sliding her hands beneath the waistband, she slipped them lower, letting out a guttural gasp of longing when she realised he was naked underneath. Her fingertips skittered over the bare skin of his buttocks, leaving a trail of goosebumps behind them, the muscles clenching tightly beneath her touch. He felt so good, so gloriously hard, tight and male that Anna realised she was panting with excitement, her breath coming in short gasps.

Sliding her hands down further, she traced the underside of his buttocks and when she firmly cupped both cheeks in her hands, squeezing them tightly with a strength born of pure need, she was rewarded with a sharp hiss of breath and a bucking movement that thrust the shape of his mighty erection against her stomach.

Anna let out a low moan. Reaching up on tiptoe, she tried to make herself as tall as possible so she could feel his erection where she so desperately wanted it—against her groin. But Zahir went one better, lifting her off her feet as if she were weightless, one ankle boot dropping to the ground with a thud. Wrapping her legs around his waist, the glorious feel of him was now pressing against her sex and she closed her eyes against the thrill as she clung dizzily to him, her arms around his neck, feeling him turn and move towards his bedroom.

She opened them again as he set her down, wobbling unsteadily on her feet as she watched him tear his shirt over his head, his breathing heavy with need. It was dark in this cave-like room, the shutters closed against the night, the bed no more than a low shape on the floor. Stripped to the waist, Zahir brought Anna towards him again, sweeping her hair over one shoulder, nuzzling her neck with his lips as his hands slid the zipper of her dress down her back.

'You want this, Anna?'

It was the same question he had asked her in the log cabin before it had all gone horribly wrong. But she wasn't going to mess it up this time. Want was too small a word to describe the fervour she felt for Zahir right now. It was an overpowering, all-consuming madness. Something she couldn't bring herself to examine. For now, a simple yes would have to suffice.

She groaned the word hotly against his shoulder as he tugged at her dress and it fell to the ground. Now he was undoing the clasp of her bra, releasing her breasts until they were caught, heavy and aching with need, by his caressing palms, his thumb stroking over nipples that had shrivelled into hard peaks. Anna's hands strayed down to his loose-fitting trousers again, tugging at them until they were low over his hips, finally falling to the ground. He was naked, the force of his erection escaping at last, throbbing between them.

'Say it again, Annalina.' He ground out the words, one hand reaching for her panties, pulling them down her legs, taking the remaining boot with them.

'I want you.'

With a guttural growl he swept her off her feet again, laying her down on the bed and positioning himself over her, his eyes shining like jet in the darkness as they raked over her face. With his jaw held fast, the sharp angles of his cheeks hollowed and shadowed, he looked magnificent. And he looked like a man on the edge.

'You're going to have to control me, Annalina.' He lowered his body until it was held fractionally above her by the flexed columns of his arms, his mouth just a centimetre from her own. 'Take me at the speed you are comfortable with.'

Anna gulped. She had totally lost control of herself—what hope did she have of controlling him? And 'comfortable' was not a word she was interested in. She wanted mind-blowing, all-consuming sex. Speech had all but deserted her but she did manage to drag up something that she suddenly knew to be true.

'I trust you, Zahir.'

This produced a stab of surprise that had his eyes widen then narrow again. Zahir hesitated, as if about to say something, then he changed his mind, moving his hand between her legs instead, pushing her thighs apart so that he could slide his fingers inside her.

Anna shuddered with pleasure at his touch, his fingers working to intensify her arousal, increase the wetness that slicked her core. As her whole body began to shake, she reached behind his back to steady herself, to stop him from moving away, her hands desperately gripping on to him. Her legs splayed wider, her back arching into his touch.

'God, Annalina. You have no idea what you do to me.' He growled deeply before he took her mouth again, his tongue licking and tasting at the same speed as his finger stroked and rubbed. 'You need to say now if you want this to stop.'

'Don't stop, Zahir. Do it—make love to me.'

'Uh-uh.' With another thickly uttered growl, Zahir withdrew his hand and, reaching for Anna's, guided it to his member, curling her fist around the silky, heated girth of him. 'You are in control, Anna. Remember that. Whatever happens now is down to you.'

Oh, dear Lord. Anna wasn't prepared for this. She had fantasised about this moment for so long, yearned, craved and ached for it almost since the first moment she had clapped eyes on Zahir. But she had stressed about it too, agonised over what might happen, the dreadful accusation that had been implanted in her mind by Henrik refusing to be totally banished. But in every imagined scenario it had been Zahir taking command, taking her any way he wanted to, dominating her the way he had when they'd been in the cabin. Not that that hadn't been indescribably, erotically mind-blowing. But it had held an element of fear too.

This was different. As she started to slide her hand up and down the thick length of him, felt him shudder beneath her touch, any traces of fear subsided. He was big, so astonishingly, eye-wateringly enormous, but she wasn't scared. Just mindlessly high with exhilaration, as if he was a drug she could never get enough of.

And she knew she was ready for him, ready in mind and body.

Shifting her bottom, she spread her legs wider, positioning the head of his shaft exactly where she wanted it. Zahir froze, not moving, not even breathing, his whole body rigid with unspoken, unleashed power. She started to make small, circling movements with him, pressing him against her most sensitive spot, small mews escaping her lips. She was so wet now, so aroused. She paused, seeking his eyes, eyes that were black with desire, as drugged and drowning as her own.

'Now, Zahir.' She whispered the command hoarsely.

He didn't need telling twice. With his arms braced on either side of her head, he lowered his hips, plunging the head of his member into Anna's wet, tight, sensitised core. Anna gasped, her muscles clenching around him, holding him firm as her legs drew up, her hands clawing at his back.

'Annalina?'

'More, Zahir. I want more.'

'Oh, God.' With a primal groan, Zahir obeyed, pushing more of his length into her with a slick, hot, juddering force. He paused again as Anna's legs clamped around him, her nails digging into his flesh.

'All of it, Zahir. I want to feel all of you.' She had no idea who this dominatrix was—who had taken over her body—just knew that the control was intoxicating, banishing her fears.

To have a man like Zahir obeying her commands was wildly exhilarating. Mind-blowing. And the feel of him inside her was indescribably, gloriously wonderful.

With one final, punishing thrust he was there, fully inside her, firmly gripped by muscles that pulsed and contracted with ripples of ecstasy. With a whimper of abandonment, Anna lifted her head and flung her arms around his neck, pulling his mouth down to meet hers, plunging her fingers into the thick mass of his hair to keep him there. With their breath and saliva mingled, their bodies sealed with sweat and joined in the most carnal of ways, Zahir began to move. Slowly at first, easing his length out of her, almost to the tip, before thrusting in again. But, as Anna urged him on with rasped, pleading words of need, he took over, the control now firmly his, pumping harder and faster, his breathing heavy and harsh, as again and again he plundered her body, each thrust bringing her further and further towards the oblivion of orgasm.

'Zahir!' She gasped his name as the tremendous sensation built and built until she could take no more, until she was at the very brink, hanging on with an agonising ecstasy that couldn't last any longer. 'Please...please...'

'Say it, Anna. What do you want?'

'You, Zahir.' Anna let out a whimper that ended in a strangled scream. 'I want you to come, now, with me.'

Her body started to shudder, trembling violently as she surrendered to the tremendous surge of sensation that flooded her from head to toe. She heard Zahir's breathing grow hoarse, felt his muscles flex and jerk as he pounded into her with the final delirious thrusts, his beautiful face contorted with the concentration and effort. For a split second he stopped, holding himself rigid, and then he was there, his orgasm intensifying hers, taking them both to unknown realms of euphoria. Anna cried out, totally lost in the moment.

But it was Zahir's primal roar that echoed round the room.

CHAPTER TWELVE

ANNA AWOKE WITH a start. The room was pitch-black and for a moment she had no idea where she was. Then in a rush she remembered: she was in Zahir's bedroom, in his bed. They had had sex—more than that, they had made love. And it had been the single most wonderful experience of her life.

She let the memory flood over her, reliving the wonder of it, the incredible coupling they had shared. The intensity of feelings she had experienced had gone far beyond just sex, or losing her virginity, or proving that there wasn't actually anything wrong with her, that she was a proper woman after all. In fact, it had gone far beyond anything she ever could have possibly imagined. Something momentous had happened between them, something very special. The floodgates had opened without permission from either of them, washing away all the anger and pride, the fears, resentment and battle for control that had been so painfully consuming them up until now. All gone on a tidal wave of unadulterated passion.

But something else had been washed away too. *The pretence.* The notion that what she felt for Zahir was simply infatuation or a wild obsession or a silly crush that she could somehow control. Because now she knew the indisputable truth. She was in love with Zahir Zahani. Deeply, desperately, dangerously in love.

Anna closed her eyes against the sheer force of the truth, powerless to do anything except accept it. She thought back to lying in Zahir's arms, sated and exhausted, to the pure pleasure of being held by him, listening to him breathing, her euphoria keeping her awake long after he had surrendered to sleep. She couldn't worry about the consequences of her love for him—at least not now, not tonight. She refused to let anything spoil this one, remarkable night.

Except maybe it was already spoiled. Stretching an arm across the crumpled sheets, she already knew that Zahir had gone. The fact that bed was still warm beside her was no consolation.

Anna held herself very still, listening. There it was again, the noise that had woken her up, a series of dull thuds coming from somewhere far away in the palace. Sitting up in bed, she pulled the covers around her shoulders. What was it? It sounded almost like a wrecking ball, a tremendous weight hitting something solid over and over again. She could hear voices now, muffled shouting, as if the whole of the palace had woken up. And then she heard the most frightening sound of all. A howl, like a wild animal, echoing through the night, and again, louder and more desperate. But what made it all the more terrifying, what made Anna cower back into the mattress, was the fact that the sound definitely came from a human.

Cautiously she got up off the bed. Now her eyes had acclimatised to the gloom, she could make out their discarded clothes scattered on the floor. She found her knickers, hastily pulled them on and was holding Zahir's shirt in her hand when another howl cut through the air. It seemed even louder this time. Suddenly finding the right clothes didn't matter. Getting out of here definitely did.

Hastily tugging Zahir's shirt over her head, she stepped out into the unlit corridor. The sounds were coming from somewhere above, harsh voices, a thumping noise like furniture being turned over, and still that horrendous howling. She knew she had to find her way back to her suite of rooms which were somewhere on the first floor but fear made her hesitate. What on earth was going on? What sort of a mad house had she come to?

Out of the corner of her eye she noticed a flight of stairs leading off the corridor to her left. They were narrow and dark but right now they seemed a better alternative to wandering into the main atrium of the palace and exposing herself to whatever hell was happening out there.

Stealthily climbing the stairs, she lifted the latch of the heavy wooden door at the top and it creaked open. She was in another corridor, wider this time, and dimly lit by wall lights. Hurriedly following what seemed like miles of passageway, her bare feet soundless on the wooden floor, Anna tried to figure out where she was, how she could find her way back to somewhere she recognised. When the corridor ended with another, grander door, she hesitated, listening for sounds on the other side. Nothing.

The howling had stopped now, along with the crashing and banging. All seemed quiet. Spookily so. She noticed that there was a key in the lock on this side of the door but the door opened easily on her turning the handle. She stepped into the room just as a strangled scream pierced the air. It took a moment to realise it had come from her.

She was standing in her own bedroom. And it had been totally trashed. The furniture had been reduced to firewood, an enormous gilt-framed mirror smashed to smithereens, glass all over the floor. The bed was in ruins, the stuffing pulled out of the mattress, the pictures on the walls punched through or hanging crazily from their hooks. Anna gazed around in speechless horror. The wardrobe was lying on its back, all her clothes wrenched from it and violently ripped to pieces, shredded by some maniacal hand. Dresses had been slashed and hurled to the ground. Tops, trousers, even her underwear, hadn't escaped the vicious attack, bras and panties torn to bits and scattered in amongst the piles of debris. It was a terrifying scene.

And in the middle of it were the two brothers—Zahir and Rashid. Rashid was crouched down, his head in his hands, silently rocking. Zahir was standing over him, wearing nothing but the same loose trousers Anna had lowered from his body a short while ago. But, as he turned to look at her, Anna heard herself scream again. His chest was smeared with blood, deep, vertical lacerations that looked as if they'd been made by some sort of animal. There were scratches all over his arms too, on the hands that he held up to ward her off.

'Get out of here, Annalina!'

But Anna couldn't move, frozen by the horror of the sight, her brain unsure if this was real or if she'd stepped into some terrible nightmare.

'I said *go*.'

No, this was real, all right. Zahir was advancing towards her now, bearing down on her with the look of a man who would not be disobeyed. Anna felt herself back away until she could feel the wall behind her.

'Wh...what has happened?' She tried to peer around Zahir's advancing body to look at Rashid, who had wrapped his arms around his knees and was still rocking back and forth.

'I'm dealing with this, Annalina.'

Zahir was right in front of her now, trying to control her with eyes that shone wild and black. She could see the thick corded veins throbbing in his neck, smell the sweat on him, sense the fight in him that he was struggling to control.

'And I am telling you to go.' Grabbing hold of her upper arms, his forceful grip biting into her soft flesh, he started to turn her in the direction she had come from. 'You are to go back to my chambers and wait for me.' When she finally nodded, he let out a breath. 'And lock the door behind you.'

She nodded again, her knees starting to shake

now as Zahir herded her towards the door. Looking over her shoulder, she took in the scene of devastation once more, the thought of the demons that must be possessing Rashid to bring about such violence, to cause such destruction, striking fear into her heart. Because Rashid had done this. She had no doubt about that.

Suddenly Rashid threw back his head. Their eyes met and there was that stare again, only this time it was far more chilling, far more deranged. She watched as he stealthily rose to his feet, hunching his shoulders and clenching his fists by his sides. Now he was starting to step silently towards them but, intent on getting Anna out of the room, Zahir hadn't seen him. With her brain refusing to process what she was seeing, it was a second before Anna let out the cry that spun him around. A second too late. Because Rashid had leapt between them, knocking her to the ground and clasping his hands around her throat. She caught the bulging madness in his eyes as the pressure increased, heard Zahir's roar echo round the room, and then the weight of a tangle of bodies on top of her followed by silence. And then nothing but darkness.

Zahir stared down at Anna's sleeping face, so pale in the glow of light from the single bedside lamp. Her hair was spread across the pillow like spun gold, like the stuff of fairy tales. *Beauty and the Beast.* Suddenly he remembered how that creature Henrik had referred to them and now he wondered if he had been right. Because Zahir had never felt more of a beast than he did now.

Seeing Rashid attack Anna had all but crucified him, the shock of it still firing through his veins. That he had let it happen, failed to protect someone dear to him *yet again*, filled him with such self-loathing that he thought he might vomit from the strength of it. And the fact that this terrible attack had made him face up to his feelings only added to his torment. Because Annalina was dear to him. Dangerously, alarmingly dear. And that meant he had to take drastic action.

Somehow he had managed to control the surge of violence towards Rashid. It had been strong enough to slay him on the spot, or at the very least punch him to the ground, the way he had with Henrik. Because that was his answer to everything, wasn't it? Violence. The only language he understood. But with Annalina still in danger he had driven that thought from his mind. Prising his brother's fingers from around her neck, he had shoved him to one side, taking the punishment of his increasingly feeble blows to his back and his head as he'd bent over Annalina, gathering her against his chest and shielding her with his body as he'd crossed the debris-strewn room and locked the door behind him. Leaving Rashid and his terrible madness inside.

Out in the corridor a doctor was already hurrying towards them. Zahir had called him earlier to attend to Rashid, before foolishly trying to go and reason with him himself. But right now Rashid would have to wait. Right now nothing mattered except Annalina. Ordering the doctor to follow him, he pounded along the corridors with Annalina in his arms, bursting into the nearest bedroom and laying her down on the bed like the most precious thing in the world. Because suddenly he realised that she was.

Her eyes were already fluttering open when the doctor bent to examine her—his verdict that the marks on her neck were only superficial, that she had most probably fainted from the shock, a massive relief before it had given way to the feelings of utter disgust towards himself.

With the doctor insisting that the only treatment Annalina needed was rest, Zahir had reluctantly left her in the care of the servants to be put to bed for what was left of the night.

Annalina was already insisting that she was fine, that she was sorry for having been such a drama queen, that he should go to Rashid to see how he was.

But Zahir returned to his chambers, having no desire to see any more of his brother tonight. He didn't trust himself—his emotions were still running far too high. And, besides, the doctor would have sedated Rashid by now. He would be blissfully unconscious. Zahir could only yearn for the same oblivion. There was no way he would sleep tonight.

So instead he took a shower, feeling a masochistic pleasure in the sting of the water as it pounded over the cuts and scratches inflicted by his brother, towelling himself dry with excessive roughness over the clawed wounds on his chest, staring at the blood on the towel, as if looking for absolution, before tossing it to the ground. Because there was no absolution to be had. Quite the reverse.

The thought that Annalina could so easily have ended up married to Rashid tore at his soul. Because the betrothal had been all his idea, his appalling lack of judgement. He had convinced himself that marriage and a family would be beneficial for Rashid, then had bullied him into agreeing to his plan.

He had told himself that his brother was getting better, that his problems would soon be solved with a bit more time and the right medication. Not because it was the truth—dear God, this evening had shown how desperately far from the truth it was—but because that was what he had wanted to believe. And not even for Rashid's sake, but for his own. To ease the weight of guilt. If it hadn't been for Annalina's courage, her bravery that night on the bridge in Paris, she would have found herself married to a dangerously unstable man. A man who clearly meant to do her harm. And that was something else Zahir could add to the growing list of things he would never forgive himself for.

The confines of his rooms felt increasingly claustrophobic as he paced around, the silence he had thought he craved so badly resonating like a death knell in his ears. And coming across Annalina's dress lying on his bedroom floor only intensified his suffering. Picking it up, he laid it across the bed, the sight of the crumpled sheets sending a bolt of twisted torment through him.

For sex with Annalina had been unlike any sexual experience Zahir had ever had before—so powerful in its intensity that it had obliterated all reason, all doubts. And, even more astonishing, afterwards he had fallen asleep, drugged by a curious contentment totally unknown to him. For Zahir had never, *ever* slept in a woman's arms. The only sex he had ever known had been perfunctory, used solely as a means of release, leaving him feeling vaguely soiled, as if debased by his own physical needs. In short, once the deed had been done, he had been out of there. But with Annalina it had been different. He had felt stronger for having made love to her, calmer, more complete. Somehow made whole. But then with Anna everything was different.

But his euphoric peace had been short-lived, shattered first by howls and then sounds of destruction that he instantly knew had to be his brother. In his haste to go to him he had abandoned Annalina, not thinking that she would follow him, that she was the one who was in danger. That she would end up being attacked.

A surge of impotent energy saw him retracing his steps back up to the bedroom where she was sleeping, startling the young servant, Lana, who for some reason had taken it upon herself to keep a bedside vigil. Curtly dismissing her, he had taken her place, the realisation of what he had to do growing with every minute that passed as he gazed down at Anna's peaceful face. He had been wrong to marry her, to bring her here. No good would ever come of it. If he wanted to protect her, he knew what he had to do. He had to set her free.

Anna opened her eyes, at first startled, then feeling her heart leap when she saw that Zahir was at her bedside, staring at her with silent intensity.

'What time is it?' She started to push herself up against the pillows. What day was it, come to that? Crossing time zones, the glorious wonder of sex with Zahir, the terror of Rashid's assault meant she had totally lost all sense of date and time. Her hand went to her throat as the dreadful memory came back. It felt slightly tender, nothing more.

'About four a.m.' Zahir shifted in his seat but his eyes never left her face.

Anna sat up further, brushing the hair away from her face. 'What are you doing here?' Something about Zahir's still demeanour, the dispassionate way he was observing her, was starting to alarm her. She moved her hand across the coverlet to find his but, instead of taking it, he folded his arms across his chest, sitting ramrod-straight in his chair. 'Is it Rashid? Has something happened to him?'

'Rashid has been sedated. He will give us no further trouble tonight.'

'Well, that's good, I suppose.'

'You should go back to sleep. The doctor said you must rest.' Zahir rose to his feet. For a moment Anna thought he was going to leave but instead he moved round to the end of the bed where he stood watching her like a dark angel. A couple of seconds of silence ticked by before he spoke again. 'Your neck.' His voice was gruff, as if he had been the one with the hands around his throat. 'Does it hurt?'

'No.' His obvious anguish made Anna want to lessen his burden. 'Honestly, I'm fine. But what about you? The marks on your chest, Zahir, they looked bad.'

'They are nothing.' He immediately closed her down. They were obviously to be covered up by more than the loose white shirt that now clad his chest.

'I'm sorry that I made the situation worse by swooning like a Victorian heroine.' She pulled an apologetic face. 'I don't know what came over me. I think it must have been the shock.'

'You have nothing to apologise for.' His hands gripped the end of the bed. 'It is I who should be sorry.'

'What happened, Zahir?' She lowered her voice. 'Why did Rashid go berserk like that?'

Zahir looked away into the darkness of the room. 'Apparently he failed to take his medication when he was in Dorrada.'

'And that…that fury was the result?' She bit down on her lip. 'But why did he target me, Zahir? Rip up *my* clothes, try to attack me? What does he have against me?'

'He had no idea what he was doing. He attacked me too, his own brother.'

'But only because you were trying to stop him from trashing my room.' She hadn't been sure until that moment, but now she saw that she was right.

'It seems he regards you as some sort of threat.' Zahir still couldn't meet her eye. 'In his deranged state, he's somehow confusing you with the person who killed our parents.'

'Oh, how awful.' Anna's heart lurched with compassion and maybe a tinge of fear. 'Poor Rashid. Maybe if I tried to speak to him—when he's calmed down, I mean.'

'No.' Now his black gaze bored into her.

'Well, is he having any other treatment, apart from medication? Counselling, for example? I'm sure there will be a doctor in Europe who could help him. I could make enquiries?' She looked earnestly across at his shadowed form.

'That won't be necessary. Rashid is my problem and I will deal with him.'

'Actually, I think he is my problem too, in view of what you've just told me… In view of what happened tonight.' Hurt at the way

Zahir curtly dismissed her offer of help hardened her voice.

'That will never happen again.'

'How can you be so sure when we're both living under the same roof?'

'Because you won't be for much longer.'

'What do you mean? Are you going to send him away?'

'No, Annalina.'

The seed of a terrible truth started to germinate. She stared at him in frozen horror.

'You're not saying…?' She swallowed past her closing throat. 'You are not intending to send *me* away?'

'I've come to the conclusion that bringing you here was a mistake.'

'A mistake?' The dead look in Zahir's eyes sent panic to her heart. 'What do you mean, a mistake?'

'I've decided that you should return to Dorrada.'

'But how can I go back to Dorrada when you are here in Nabatean?' She spoke quickly, trying to drown out the scream in her head. 'I am your wife. I should be by your side.'

'That was a mistake too.' A terrible chill cloaked the room. 'The marriage will be annulled.'

'No!' She heard the word echo around them.

'I have made up my mind, Annalina.'

This wasn't possible...it couldn't be happening. Pulling back the covers, Anna scrambled across the bed until she landed in front of Zahir with a small thump. He took a step back but the desperation in her eyes halted his retreat. He didn't mean it. He couldn't be ending their marriage, casting her aside just like that. *Could he?* But one look at the determined set of his jaw, the terrible blackness of his eyes, told her that he could. And he was.

Anna clasped her hands on either side of her head as if to stop it exploding. Had she failed again so spectacularly that Zahir was prepared to end their marriage without even giving it a chance? And to do it now—when she had only just accepted how deeply she had fallen in love with him—felt like the cruellest, most heartbreaking twist of all. Seconds passed before one small question found its way through the choking fog.

'But what about last night?' She despised herself for the pitiful bleat in her voice as she searched his face for a flicker of compassion. 'Did that not mean anything to you?'

His jaw clenched in response, the shadowed planes of his handsome face hardening still further in the dim light. A twitching muscle in his cheek was the only sign of insubordination.

'Legally it will make the marriage more difficult to annul, that's true.' He raised his hand to his jaw, pressing his thumb against the rebellious muscle. 'But I'm sure it can be arranged for a price.'

Was she hearing right? Had the single most wonderful experience of her life meant nothing to Zahir? Or, worse still, had she got it so wrong, somehow been such a failure without realising it, that he would pay any price to be rid of her?

'I don't understand.' She tried again, her voice cracking as she reached forward, placing the palm on her hand on his chest, as if trying to find the heart in him, make it change Zahir's mind for her. *Make him love her.* But instead all she found was unyielding bone and taut muscle concealed beneath the cotton shirt. 'Why are you doing this?'

'I've told you. Our marriage should never have taken place. It was an error of judgement on my part. I accept full responsibility for that and am now taking steps to rectify the situation.'

'And what about me?' Her voice was little more than a whisper. 'Do I have no say in the matter?'

'No, Annalina. You do not.'

Anna turned away in a daze of unshed tears.

So this was it, then. Once more she was at the mercy of a man's decisions. Once more she was being rejected, pushed away for being inadequate. Not by her father this time, with his frozen heart, or Henrik, with his selfish needs. But Zahir. Her Zahir. Her only love.

The pain ripping through her was so fierce that she thought she might fold from the strength of it. But seconds passed and she found she was still standing, still breathing. She forced herself to think.

Clearly Zahir wasn't going to change his mind. The whole mountain of his body was drawn taut with resolve, grim determination holding him stock-still in the gloom of the room. She could beg. The idea certainly crossed her mind, desperation all too ready to push aside any dignity, pride or self-respect. But ultimately she knew it would be pointless. Zahir would not be moved, emotionally or practically. She could see that the decision had already taken root in the bedrock of his resolve. So that left only one course of action. She would leave. And she would leave right now.

Turning away, she ran into the middle of the room, but then stopped short, suddenly realising she had no clothes to wear. Her entire wardrobe had been ripped to shreds, along with her heart and soul. She looked down at the nightdress she was wearing. Lana had found it for her. She remembered her tenderly removing Zahir's shirt, remembered seeing the blood smeared across it from where he had held her to his chest, before Lana had slipped this plain cotton gown over her shaking body and helped her into bed.

But she could hardly go out dressed like this. Covering her face with her hands, she tried to decide what to do. The clothes that she had travelled in what seemed like several centuries ago now were scattered somewhere in Zahir's chambers. Much as she dreaded going back there, she had no alternative.

Turning on her heel, she set off, fighting back the tears as she hurtled down the corridors, down the stairs, Zahir following right behind her.

'What do you think you're doing?'

Anna quickened her pace, grateful that for once her sense of direction wasn't letting her down. She recognised this corridor. She knew where she was.

'I'm going to collect my clothes from your rooms and then I'm leaving.'

'Not tonight, you're not.' He was right by her shoulder, effortlessly keeping pace with her.

'Yes, tonight.' She had reached his door

now, flinging it open, relieved to find it wasn't locked. She marched into his bedroom, switching on the light, hardly able to bring herself to look at the room that such a short space of time ago had been the scene of such joy. There was her dress, laid out on the bed like a shed skin, a previous incarnation. She rushed over to it, struggling to pull the nightgown over her head, not caring that apart from a pair of panties she was naked—that Zahir, who was standing silently in the doorway, was watching her every move, branding her bare skin with his eyes.

What did it matter? What did any of it matter now?

Stepping into the dress, she tugged up the back zipper as far as she could then cast around looking for her boots. Finding one, she clutched it to her chest and headed for the door, desperate to get out of this hateful den of misery while she still had the strength and the breath to do it.

But Zahir stood in the doorway, blocking her way.

'There is no need for this, Annalina.' Anna felt the searing heat of his hand wrap around her upper arm.

'On the contrary, there is every need.' She jerked her arm but it only made his grip tighten still further. 'Do you seriously think I would stay here a moment longer? Now I know that I am nothing more than a *mistake*, an *error of judgement*?' The words fell from her mouth like shards of glass.

'You will stay here until the morning.' He looked down at her, eyes wild and black, his heavy breath, like that of an angry bull, fanning the top of her head. 'I am not letting you leave while you're in this hysterical state.'

Hysterical state? The sheer injustice of his words misted her eyes red. Didn't she have every right to be hysterical? Didn't she have the right to scream and rant and rave—join Rashid in his madness, in fact—after the way Zahir had treated her tonight?

Yanking herself free from his clutch, she ducked under his arm and into the outer room, seizing her other boot and hopping from foot to foot as she pulled them on.

'I'll tell you what's hysterical, Zahir.' She spoke over her back, refusing to look at him. 'Me thinking that we could ever make a go of this marriage.' She straightened up, flinging her hair over her shoulders as her eyes darted around, searching for her bag and her phone. 'That we could be a proper couple, partners, lovers. That I could be a good wife to you. That what we did last night…a few hours ago…whenever the hell it was…' she choked on a rising sob '...was actually something very special.'

She stopped, making herself drag in a ragged breath before she passed out completely, shaking with misery, rage and the miserable injustice of it all.

But suddenly, there in the darkest moment, she saw the gleam of truth. Suddenly she realised she had nothing to lose any more. The barriers between them had all come down, were flattened, destroyed. There was no reason to keep the very worst agony to herself any longer.

'And do you want to know the most hysterical thing of all?' She spun around now, pinning him to the spot with the truth of her stare, letting the rush of abandonment take control of her.

'I'm in love with you, Zahir.' A harsh laugh caught in her throat, coming out as a strangled scream. 'How totally *hysterical* is that?'

CHAPTER THIRTEEN

ZAHIR FELT THE words drive through him like a knife in his guts. *She was in love with him?* How was that even possible?

He stared back in numbed silence at the flushed cheeks, the glazed eyes, the tousled blonde hair that fell down over her heaving breasts.

He longed to go to her, to break the spell, to pin her down, literally there on the floor where she stood blinking up at him. He wanted to make her say the words again, to feel them against his lips as he devoured her, made love to her again. But instead he hardened his heart. If it was true that she loved him, then that was all the more reason for him to do the right thing, the only thing, and set her free. Before he dragged her down, weakened her, destroyed her, the way he did anyone who was unfortunate enough to care for him. He simply couldn't bear that to happen to Anna.

'Well?' Finally she spoke, her voice sounding hollow, empty. 'Do you have nothing to say?'

Zahir wrestled with his conscience, with his heart, with every damned part of his body that yearned to go to her.

'It makes no difference to my decision, if that's what you mean.' His damning words were delivered with a cruel coldness born of bitter, desperate frustration. He watched as Annalina's lovely face twitched, then crumpled, her lip trembling, her eyes glittering with the sheen of tears. He deliberately made himself watch the torture, because that was what it was. He had to feel the punishment in order to keep strong.

'So…' She pushed her hair away from her face with a shaky hand. 'This is it, then?' She spoke quietly, almost as if she was asking the question of herself. But her eyes held his, the pupils dilated, like twin portals to her soul.

Zahir looked away. He couldn't witness this, not even in the name of punishment.

He sensed Annalina hesitate for a second, then heard a rustle and turned to see her slinging her bag over her shoulder and marching towards the door. A roar of frustration rang in his ears and he closed his eyes, digging his nails into the palms of his clenched fists. He would allow himself the indulgence of a couple of minutes of the agony before setting off after her.

She was at the main entrance when he caught up with her, tugging furiously at the handle of the door that was securely locked, becoming ever more desperate as she heard him approach.

'You are not leaving like this, Annalina.' He stood behind her, solid, implacable.

'No? Just try and stop me.'

'And where exactly do you think you're going, and how are you going to get there?'

'I don't know and I don't care.' She was banging her fists against the panelled door now. 'And don't pretend you care either. This is what you want, isn't it? To be rid of me as soon as possible? I'll find someone to take me to the airport and then you need never see me again.'

Reaching over her shoulder, Zahir covered her flailing fists with one hand, but Annalina pulled them away from under him.

'I mean it, Zahir. I can't stay here a minute longer. I'm leaving now.'

'Very well.' Pulling his phone from his pocket, he made a call, punching in the code of the wall safe to retrieve the keys to both the front door and his SUV as he waited for the reply. He opened a wall cupboard, taking out a coat and passing it to Anna without meeting her eye.

She was right. This was what he had told her he wanted: her gone, out of his life. The fact that it was tearing him apart only proved his point. Proved what a lethally dangerous combination they were. 'I will drive you to the airport myself.'

Anna listened as he ordered the jet to be put on standby, silently taking the coat from him before he unlocked the door and ushered her out into the cold night air. So it was really happening. She was to be banished. Cast aside like the worthless acquisition that he obviously thought she was.

Once inside the powerful SUV, she was grateful for the feeling of paralysis that had come over her, as if her body was protecting her the best it could by rendering her almost comatose. She couldn't look at Zahir, in the same way that he couldn't look at her. Instead he focussed with leaden concentration on manoeuvring the vehicle out of the electric gates that swung open for them.

They drove in total silence, Anna fighting to hold on to the merciful state of the numbness, frightened it could so easily thaw into a tidal wave of grief if she let it. She felt weighted down by the sense of him all around her, the invisible pressure bearing down on her shoulders, ringing in her ears. She stared through the windscreen, at the world that was still there, seemingly impervious to her heartbreak. Dawn was starting to break, a thread of orange lining the horizon in front of them.

The car sped silently towards it, the orange glow spreading rapidly as the peep of the sun appeared, tingeing the wispy clouds pink against the baby-blue of the sky, blackening the desert below it.

The headlights picked up the sign for the airport as they flashed past. Soon they would be there. Soon she would be leaving this country, presumably never to return. For some reason, that realisation felt like another body blow, as if someone had kicked her in the guts when she was already writhing on the ground.

She bit down on her lip, twisted her hands in her lap and fought madly to stop the tears from falling as she stared fixedly ahead at the unfolding drama of the dawn. Sunrise over the desert—one of nature's most spectacular displays.

Suddenly Anna wanted to experience it, to be a part of it. Not from here, from the agonising confines of the car, but out in the open with the cold air against her skin and the freedom to breathe it in, to be able look all around her, lean back and let the majesty unfold above her head. She needed to prove to herself that there was wonder and beauty to be had in this world, no matter how it might feel right now. If she was leaving this remarkable land for ever, she wanted one lasting memory that wasn't all about sorrow and heartbreak.

She turned her head, steeling herself to break the brittle silence, the sight of Zahir's harsh profile spawning a fresh onslaught of pain. His Adam's apple moved as he swallowed, the only visible sign that he was aware of her gaze.

'Stop the car.'

Zahir's hands tightened on the steering wheel as he shot her a wild-eyed glance.

'What?'

'I want you to stop the car. Please.'

'Why?' Alarm sounded in his voice as his eyes flashed from the road to her face and back again. 'Are you ill?'

'No, not ill.' Anna shifted in her seat. 'I want to watch the sunrise.' She tipped her chin, fighting to hold it steady, swallowing down the catch in her voice. 'Before I leave Nabatean for good, I would like to see the sunrise over the desert.'

She saw Zahir's flicker of surprise before the brows drew together, lowering to a scowl.

There was a second's silence as the car continued to speed onward.

'Very well.' His jaw tightened. 'But not here. I will find a more advantageous view.'

Anna sat back, releasing a breath she didn't even know she'd been holding in. She had no doubt that Zahir would know exactly where to take them. It seemed to her that he knew every grain of sand of this desert, that it was a part of him, of who he was, wild and bleak.

Sure enough, a short while later he swung the vehicle off the main road, bumping it over the rough terrain, and almost immediately they appeared to have left civilisation completely and become part of the barren wilderness of the desert. Zahir pushed the SUV hard, bouncing it over the hard ridges of compacted sand at great speed, navigating along a dried-up riverbed before swinging off to the right and powering up the side of a dune the size of a small mountain.

Beside him Anna clung to her seat, grateful for the mad recklessness of the journey that temporarily obliterated all other thoughts. Finally they skidded to a halt with a spray of sand and she peered through the speckled windscreen, seeing nothing but the grey shadowed desert. Abruptly getting out of the car, Zahir came round and opened her door for her.

'We will need to do the last bit on foot.' He held out his hand but Anna ignored it, jumping down unaided and focussing on nothing but this one goal as she followed Zahir up the towering peak of the dune, her thighs aching as she tried to keep up with him, her boots sinking into the shifting sand. Ahead of her Zahir had stopped to hold out his hand again and this time Anna took it, feeling herself being pulled up onto the very top of the dune. And into another world.

If it was wondrous beauty that she wanted, here it was, spread out before her. The sky was on fire with oranges, reds and yellows, the horizon a vivid slash of violet, the colours so amazingly vibrant that they looked to have been splashed from a children's paint box. Before them the dunes rolled like waves of the sea, washed pink by the fast-rising sun that highlighted the thousands of rippled ridges with finely detailed shadows.

Anna dropped to her knees and just stared and stared, intent on blocking everything else out, storing this image so that it would be there for ever. She didn't even notice the tears that were starting to fall.

Zahir cast his eyes down to where Annalina knelt beside him, her profile glowing amber in the light of the sun. The sight of the tears rolling unchecked down her cheeks threatened to undo him so completely that he had to look away. Whatever had he been thinking, bringing her here? What madness had made him want to prolong the torture? He scowled, channelling his agony into determination. He had to be cruel to be kind.

Minutes passed with no sound except the occasional cry of a bird, the rustle of the wind as it danced across the sand, the beat of his pulse in his ears. He had never known Annalina to be so silent, so still. The soft breeze that lifted her hair went unnoticed. It almost felt as if she had left him already. He pushed the sharp pain of that thought away and, staring out at the barren landscape, sought to find some words to end this agony.

'This is for your own good, Annalina.' He forced the words past the jagged blades in his throat. 'After what happened with Rashid, it is clear that you can no longer stay here.'

He saw her twitch inside the coat that she had pulled tight around her body. But she remained infuriatingly silent.

'And besides.' Her refusal to agree with him only made him more coldly determined, crueller. 'This is no place for you. You don't belong here and you never will.'

'Is that so?' She spoke quietly into the cold, new day, still refusing to look at him.

'Yes. It is.'

'And now I will never be given the chance to prove otherwise.' She hunched her shoulders, still staring straight ahead. 'By banishing me, you're simply confirming your assumptions. You're shoring up your own prejudices.'

'I am doing no such thing.' He heard himself roar his reply. Raising a hand, he covered his eyes, squeezing his temples to take away the anger and the pain. Why did she persist in arguing like this, goading him? Or had he provoked the reaction—in which case, why? He was certainly regretting it now. 'That is not true.'

'No? Are you sure, Zahir?' He could hear her fighting to control the tremor in her voice. 'Because that's what it feels like to me. There is no reason for me to leave Nabatean. We could find some help for Rashid—intensive psychiatric counselling. We could focus on making our relationship work, on building a future together.' She turned to give him a look full of scorn but beneath the scorn was hurt, that terrible hurt. 'But, what you really mean is, you don't want me here.'

Zahir forced himself to watch as she turned back, roughly brushing away the tears and biting down on her lip to steady it. He wanted her to stay more than he had ever wanted anything in his life. But he could not let her see that. He could not let his lack of judgement jeopardise her safety any more than it had already. Let his own desires compromise her well-being. More than that, he could not let his *selfishness* crush the life out of this precious creature. Because that was what would happen if she put her happiness in his hands.

'Very well.' He hardened his heart until it felt like lump of stone inside him. 'Since you put it that way, you are right. I don't want you here.' It crucified him to say the words, but say them he had to. 'The sooner you leave, the better for all concerned.'

She flinched as if he had struck her, and Zahir experienced the same horror, as if he had done just that.

'Well, thank you for the truth.' Finally she spoke, her words floating softly into the air before the dreadful silence wrapped itself around them again.

Zahir looked over his shoulder. He couldn't take any more of this. 'We need to get going.' He paced several steps across the top of the dune, glancing back to where Annalina hadn't moved. 'The crew will have the jet ready for take-off.'

He didn't give a damn about the jet or the crew. He just knew he had get away from here, deliver Annalina to the airport and put an end to this agony.

'In a minute.' She spoke with icy clarity. 'First I would like a little time alone. You go back to the car.'

Curbing the desire to tell her that he was the one who gave the orders around here, and that furthermore he expected her to obey them, Zahir drew in a steadying breath. Certainly there was no way he was going to leave her up here on her own. 'Five minutes, then.' He looked around them, pointing his finger. 'I will wait for you over there.'

Anna watched as he strode away, the breeze billowing the loose fabric of his trousers as he climbed up onto the next dune and stood there with his hands on his hips, tall and dark against the skyline.

The shock of his rejection had hardened now, the misery solidifying inside her until it felt less like a bad dream and more like leaden reality. The way Zahir had so callously dismissed her declaration of love still threatened to flay her skin but now she saw that it had been inevitable. A man such as Zahir would never be able to graciously accept such a sentiment. He didn't know how. His own heart was too neglected. It was buried too deep.

She was staring into the crimson wash of the sky when a sudden thought came to her, dawning like the new day. It trickled slowly at first, but soon started to warm her, to heat her from within, until she began to throb with the idea of it—whether through hope, desperation or fear she didn't know. If Zahir's heart was so buried, so unreachable, perhaps it was up to her to try and change that.

Perhaps it was her duty to try and find it.

Zahir watched as Annalina got to her feet, expecting to see her start the descent back to the car. But instead she was heading towards him, scrambling over the sand that was shifting beneath her feet in her hurry to reach him. He saw her stumble and instinctively started to go to her but she was up on her feet again, using her hands now to propel herself forward until she had reached the top of the dune and pulled herself up beside him.

'I know you don't want to hear it but I'm going to say it again anyway.' Her words came out all of a rush as her breath rasped in her throat, her chest heaving beneath the padded coat. 'I love you, Zahir.' She gulped painfully. 'And nothing you can say or do will ever alter that.'

She was staring at him now, her hair blowing around her flushed cheeks, those beautiful blue eyes searching his face, beseeching him. Why? For what reason? He didn't even know.

'Love has no place here.' He struggled wildly to release himself from her gaze, from the grip of her declaration. But when that bleak statement didn't work, when she still refused to look away, he tried again, desperately searching for some sort of logic to make her see sense.

'Besides, I suspect it is no more than an aberration.' He tried to soften his voice, to sound reasonable, even though he had never felt less reasonable, more cut loose from sanity, in his life. 'When you return to your country, you will see that.'

'This is no aberration, Zahir.' Stubbornly she refused to back down. 'I will do as you say. I will get on that plane and fly back to Dorrada. But I guarantee it will change nothing, no matter how much you want it to. Neither time nor distance nor death itself will change how I feel. I love you, Zahir. And I always will.'

Zahir closed his eyes against the astonishingly punishing power of her words. He couldn't accept them. He refused to accept them. A beautiful creature such as Annalina could never truly love a brute like him. He struggled to try and find the words to explain that to her, cursing when they refused to come to him, as if his vocabulary was deliberately defying him.

'And what's more…' She held the moment in her hand, poised for the final thrust. 'I think that you love me too.'

CHAPTER FOURTEEN

ANNA SAW HIM FLINCH, felt the twist of it inside her. She had no idea if it was true. It was as deranged a notion as it was incredible. The tortured look on Zahir's face told her nothing either, except that her rash words had affected him deeply. But it was worth a try. What did she have to lose? Certainly not her pride—there was precious little of that left to worry about. And self-respect? If that was hanging by a thread too maybe it was time to stand up for herself, to challenge Zahir's decision. All her life she had been the victim of other people's schemes and machinations. Well enough. This time she was going to fight for what *she* wanted. She was going to fight for the man she loved.

'Zahir?' Gathering her courage around her, she broke the silence softly, like popping a bubble in the air. 'Do you have nothing to say?' She stretched out a hand to his face, turning him towards her. 'Look at me, Zahir. Tell me what you're feeling.'

'I see no purpose in that.' He turned against her hand, his stubbled jaw rough against her fingers as he presented her with his most harsh profile.

'Tell me why you flinch when I talk about love.' Still Anna persisted. 'What is it about the idea that frightens you so much?'

This spun his head back round, made her drop her hands from his cheeks. The notion of Zahir being frightened of anything was totally ridiculous and yet, as she searched his furious gaze, she could see that it was true.

'I have no idea what love is,' he fired back. 'It is beyond my reasoning.'

'No, Zahir. I don't believe you. I could hear the love in your voice when you spoke to me of your mother. I can see it in the patience you show to Rashid. You are capable of love, no matter how much you want to deny it.'

'And look what happened to them, to my parents, to Rashid.' He let out a cry that echoed around them. 'Look what happens to the people that you claim I love. They are either murdered or left mentally deranged. Is that what you want for yourself, Annalina?

'Stop this, Zahir!' She matched his cry. 'You

can't go on blaming yourself for what happened for ever.'

'I can and I will.'

'Then so be it.' She knew there would be no changing his mind when it came to that terrible night. The guilt was too deep-rooted, too all-encompassing. 'But you have no right to punish me for it as well.'

'You!' His eyes flashed with fire. 'Can't you see I'm trying to protect you, not punish you? I'm trying to save you from the hideous consequences of falling in love with me.'

'It's too late for that. And, even if it weren't, I would be prepared to take the risk if there was any possibility that you might return my love.'

'Really? Then you are a fool. Because misery is the only reward you will get from such a return.'

'No, I am not a fool, Zahir. I love you.' She countered his temper with calm assertion, pressing down on the tightly coiled spring inside her to stop it from wreaking unimaginable havoc. 'I think I have always loved you, from the very first moment we met. It is an emotion out of my control. There is absolutely nothing I can do about it.'

She paused, her eyes trained on his, refusing even to blink. 'Up until the time we made love, only a few short hours ago, I would never have dared to think that you might love me too. But I felt the heat of your body as you touched me, heard your cry of release when you came, listened to the beat of your heart as you fell asleep with me in your arms. And that has given me hope.

'So, if there is any chance that you might love me too, then I'm going to drag it out of you. It doesn't have to make any difference to our relationship. I will still leave for Dorrada, if that's what you want. I will agree to the annulment of the marriage, sever all contact with you for ever, if you truly believe that's how it has to be. But, if you feel any love for me, I believe I have the right to be told.'

Zahir felt Anna's impassioned speech rock the very foundation of his being, dislodging the corner stone that kept him upright, made him the man he was. He could feel himself wobble, threatening to tumble like a pile of building blocks at her feet.

All his life he had been so sure of his focus. His beloved country had been what mattered. That was at the heart of everything he did, including the reason he had married Annalina and brought her here. But his judgement had been flawed, and not for the first time. Now she was challenging his decision to release her, pushing and pushing, messing with his head until he no longer knew right from wrong any more. Her declaration of love, delivered with such composure, had ripped him wide open. And now she seemed determined to make him stare into the very depths of his own heart.

He looked down at her beautiful, open face, so moved by her words that he couldn't think straight. He wanted to be able to formulate some sort of reply but nothing would come, his throat choked with something that felt alarmingly like tears. Turning his head away, he swallowed madly.

'Zahir?' She reached for him again, taking his face in her hands and holding it firmly in her cold grip, her gaze raking mercilessly over every tortured inch of it. Zahir tried to blink, to look away, but it was too late. She had already seen the sheen in his eyes. 'Oh, Zahir!'

Raising herself up, she touched his lips with her own, nudging them with the gentlest feather-light pressure. 'Say it. Say it to me now.'

'No!' Her breath was a soft whisper on his skin but still he fought off its assault. Anger was beginning to surge through him now at the way she was clawing at his masculinity, delving into his soul. That he, Zahir Zahani, the warrior prince, had been almost reduced to tears by this young woman was unthinkable. He would not stand for it. 'I will not say it. I cannot.'

'Why, Zahir? Because it isn't true? Or because you refuse to accept it?'

'Either, both, I don't know.' Screwing up his eyes, he wrenched her hands from his face and took a step back. 'This subject is now closed. We are going back to the car.'

'No, not yet.' Still she persisted, her feet firmly planted in front of him. 'I'm not going anywhere until I have seen you let yourself open up to the possibility of the truth.'

Zahir scowled at her through the slits of his eyes. 'And what the hell does that mean?'

'It means that I want you to promise that you will sit and let yourself feel. Just this once. Just for me. I want you to banish the pride, the fear or whatever else it is that's holding you back and let the truth come through. Set it free. Whatever that truth is, I will accept it and I will never ask you to speak it again. But you owe me this one thing, Zahir.'

Zahir hesitated. If this hippy nonsense meant that she would finally release him, end this terrible inquisition, then maybe he would do it. 'Very well.' He watched as Annalina moved away to give him some space, sitting herself down and hugging her knees, her focus straight ahead. Suddenly it was just him and the sparkling clarity of the new day. There was nowhere to hide.

He let his eyelids drop. Presumably this was what she expected of him so he would play along. He breathed in and out, letting his shoulders drop, the arms that were folded so tightly across his chest loosen. He felt himself relax.

Annalina. The spirit of her came out of nowhere, filling his head, his heart, his whole body. He tried to fight against it, against the witchcraft, black magic or whatever spell it was that she had cast over him, but it was hopeless. Suddenly he was exposed, laid bare, everything he had been denying, blocking out, pushing away, presented before him with bruising clarity. And, more than that, as if a tap was being turned on inside him he could feel the empty vessel that he had once been filling, gushing and gushing until he was almost drowning from the flood of it, gasping for air. And then it was too late, he had no control any more, and the wave crashed over him. And suddenly he recognised the phenomenon for what it was: the acceptance of love.

Beside her Anna felt Zahir move, closing the gap between them until he was in front of her, standing so tall that he blotted out the rising sun. She forced her eyes slowly to travel up the length of his body but they halted at his chest, the terrible fear of what she might see refusing to let them go to his face. She was wrong. He didn't love her. It was a crazy, stupid idea, born of desperation and the blindness of her own feelings.

'Anna?' He stretched out his hands to her and she took hold of them, letting herself be pulled to standing. It was the first time she had heard him shorten her name. 'Please forgive me.' She felt her heart stutter with panic as his eyes sought hers, the near-black intensity impossible to read.

'Just now I called you a fool, but now I see that I am the fool.' He spoke softly but with grim determination. 'Now I see that what I took for strength and responsibility was actually bullying and intimidation. Never once did I allow myself to stop and look at you for who you really are because that would have exposed my own weakness.' He looked down at their joined hands then back to her face.

'For not only are you beautiful, Annalina—the most remarkable, extraordinary woman that I have ever met—but you are also brave. So much braver than me. Somehow you found the courage to declare your feelings for me, even in the face of my callous hostility. Whereas I…' He paused, the effort of overthrowing a lifetime of crippling detachment evident from the glitter in the depths of his eyes. 'I was too scared to examine how I felt for fear of what I would find there. A man who was unworthy of you in every way, who could never hope to earn your affection, let alone your love. I thought your love was far beyond anything I could ever deserve and that is why I dismissed it so cruelly. And the reason why I beg your forgiveness.'

'There is nothing to forgive, really.' Suddenly Anna didn't want to hear any more. If this was Zahir letting her down gently it was even more unbearably painful than his cold-blooded disregard. 'You don't have to explain any further.'

'Oh, but I do.' He brought her hands to his chest, clasping them against his heart. 'I have been callous and I have been cruel. By sending you away I thought I was protecting you from my brother but in reality I was only protecting myself, my own heart. But your courage has stripped away that defence and made me see what was there all along. And that is this.' He paused, raking in a breath that came from deep, deep within his soul. 'I love you, Annalina. I think I always have and I know I always will.'

For a second Anna let the words sink in, feeling them spread through her body with a ripple of pleasure that grew and grew until she thought she might explode with the joy of it. Then, throwing herself forward, she fell against him, revelling in the glorious strength of his arms as they wrapped around her, holding her so tightly against him. For several precious heartbeats they stayed locked in this embrace until Zahir loosened his hold and pulled back so that he could take her face in his hands.

'My most precious Annalina. You have shone light into my darkness, filled a void that I didn't know was there, stirred a heart that didn't know how to beat. And you have even made me find the words to tell you that.' He smiled now, the most wonderful, tender smile, and Anna felt the warmth of it flood over her, filling her to the brim with love. 'If you will have me, I am yours for ever more.'

'Oh, yes, I will have you.' With his features blurred by tears, Anna let her fingers trace the familiar contours of his face. 'And what's more, Zahir, I will never, ever let you go.'

Zahir gave a primal groan, lowering his head until he found her lips and immediately the arousal leapt between them, just as it always did. Just as it had that very first time when Anna had forced him to kiss her on the bridge in Paris. As the kiss deepened their bodies melted, moulding into one another, becoming one.

And all around them the new day burst into life.

'I have something for you.' Coming up behind her, Zahir spoke softly into the ear exposed by the swept-up tresses of Anna's intricate hairstyle.

Anna turned to look up at him, catching her breath at the stunning sight of her husband in Eastern clothes. He was wearing a long cream *shirwani* with a stand-up collar and a single row of buttons down the front and loose dark-red trousers beneath. He looked more impossibly handsome than any man had a right to be. Because he was.

Lana and Layla, who had been tweaking the folds of Anna's splendid red-and-gold gown, respectfully stepped back into the shadows of the dressing room.

'I don't think you should be here.' Anna smiled into his serious eyes, her mild rebuke melting like a wafer on her tongue. 'Isn't it supposed to be unlucky to see me before the ceremony?'

'We make our own luck, *aziziti*. Besides, this is blessing, not a wedding. I don't believe the same rules apply.'

'And even if they did I doubt very much whether you would obey them.'

'It is true that I would never obey a rule that kept me away from you.' His solemn words, accompanied by the furrowed brow, threatened to turn Anna's bones to jelly once again. That would teach her for trying to be flippant.

These past few weeks had been the most wonderful, magical time imaginable. With Zahir permitting himself some rare free time, they had scarcely left each other's sides, travelling around Nabatean so that he could show off his country, finding secret hideaways that only he knew about—a shaded oasis in the desert or ancient caves with prehistoric paintings on the walls, where he would show off something rather more private, and definitely more thrilling.

She had watched him as he worked too, patiently explaining the procedures he was involved with or taking her to meetings where he made sure that her views were respected, his obvious respect for her opinions filling her with pride. But it was the nights that had been the most special. Exploring each other's bodies in the dark, finding new ways to bring each other to soaring heights of ecstasy, before finally falling asleep in a tangle of sweat-sealed limbs. Anna marvelled at how they could never seem to get enough of one another, rejoicing in the fact that they would never have to. Because this was just the start of their lifetime together.

'So what is it, then—this something you have for me?' Tamping down the curl of longing, she smiled up at him.

'Um…it's just this.'

She watched as he felt in his pocket, producing a blue velvet ring box. He was nervous, she realised, definitely out of his very masculine comfort zone. And that made her love him all the more. He opened the lid of the box and offered it to her, almost shyly.

'Zahir!' Anna gasped at the sight of the sapphire ring, the stunning stone set in platinum and surrounded by a circle of diamonds. 'It is absolutely beautiful. Thank you!'

'I'm glad you like it. I thought the colour would match your eyes.' He gave a small cough, clearly ill at ease. 'Consider it a late engagement ring. I've noticed that you never wear the other one.'

'No.' Now it was Anna's turn to feel uncomfortable. 'I'm sorry, but…'

'You don't need to apologise, or explain.' Zahir interrupted her, taking her hand and slipping the ring onto her finger where it sat so perfectly, felt so right, that Anna could only stare at it, brimming with happiness. 'The other ring was never meant for us. By rights it should be somewhere in the mud at the bottom of the Seine. In fact…' He flashed her a mischievous grin. 'If you like, I will take you back to Paris and you can finish what you started and chuck the thing in.'

'No!' Anna raised her eyes from admiring her ring and placed her hands gently on his shoulders. 'I've got a much better idea. We will keep it safe for Rashid until he finds someone to love, someone who will make him the perfect wife.'

'Do you think that will ever happen?'

'Of course. He has only being undergoing treatment with Dr Meyer for a week but I understand that he's already making tremendous progress.'

'And I have you to thank for that, *aziziti*. For forcing me to swallow my pride and accept proper help for him. For using your contacts in Europe to find the very best doctor for him. Thank you so much.'

'Think nothing of it. Seeing Rashid return from Germany having banished his demons is the only thanks I want. And it will happen. I am sure of it.'

'You know what? I'm sure of it too.' Zahir took her hands and pressed them to his lips.

'You are the most wonderful, remarkable woman, Princess Annalina Zahani. Have I ever told you that?'

'Once or twice, I think.' Anna put her head on one side thoughtfully. 'But a girl can never receive too many compliments.'

'Hmm… Well, maybe I'll save them until after the ceremony. We don't want your head getting too big for that tiara thing, now, do we?'

He glanced across to where Lana was still patiently waiting with the jewelled headdress in her hands.

'I guess not.' Leaning forward, Anna kissed him on the lips then, turning her head, whispered in his ear. 'And I will save something for you until after the ceremony too.'

Pulling away, their eyes met, Anna's wicked twinkle dancing across Zahir's heated gaze. 'In that case, my princess, I suggest we start the ceremony without further ado. Suddenly I find I am rather impatient.'

'Suddenly I find that I agree with you.'

Sitting down just long enough for Lana to secure the headdress, Anna rose majestically to her feet and, linking her arm through Zahir's, the couple prepared to leave for the throne room.

'I love you, Annalina Zahani.' They started

walking, perfectly in step, towards their future together.

'I love you too, Zahir Zahani.'

Somewhere behind them Lana and Layla sighed with delight.

* * * * *

If you enjoyed this Andie Brock story,
why not try her other great reads
THE SHOCK CASSANO BABY
THE SHEIKH'S WEDDING CONTRACT
THE LAST HEIR OF MONTERRATO
Available now!

Also, look out for these other
WEDLOCKED! *stories*

A DIAMOND FOR DEL RIO'S HOUSEKEEPER
by Susan Stephens

BABY OF HIS REVENGE
by Jennie Lucas
Available now!